GHOSTS OF
ST. AUGUSTINE

GHOSTS OF

Dave Lapham

ILLUSTRATED BY TOM LAPHAM

 PINEAPPLE PRESS, INC.
SARASOTA, FLORIDA

Inquiries should be addressed to:
Pineapple Press, Inc.
P.O. Box 3899
Sarasota, Florida 34230

Library of Congress Cataloging in Publication Data

Lapham, Dave, 1939–
    Ghosts of St. Augustine / Dave Lapham ; illustrated by Tom Lapham.
        p. cm.
    Includes bibliographical references.
    ISBN 1-56164-123-5 (alk. paper)
    1. Ghosts—Florida—Saint Augustine.   2. Ghosts stories—Florida—Saint
Augustine.   I. Title.
GR110.F5L36   1997
398.2'09759'1805—dc21   96-49882
                                         CIP

First Edition
10 9 8 7 6 5 4 3

Design by Carol Tornatore
Printed and bound by Edwards Brothers, Ann Arbor, Michigan

To the friendly and gracious folk of

St. Augustine,

those living and those dead,

and to my long-suffering wife,

Sue

CONTENTS

ACKNOWLEDGMENTS

A SPECIAL THANKS TO SANDY CRAIG of Tour of St. Augustine, who provided contacts, stories of her own, and encouragement. I value her friendship.

Thanks also to Karen Harvey for the information, support, and contacts she provided and to Katie Arnold of the Booksmith who introduced me to countless people and who urged me on.

And, finally, my appreciation to all the wonderful people of the Ancient City who have offered me their stories and their hospitality.

In gathering the stories I referred often to *The Oldest City*, edited by Jean Parker Waterbury, St. Augustine Historical Society, St. Augustine, FL, 1983; a series of five articles by Karen Harvey which appeared in the *Compass* magazine of the *St. Augustine Record* between May 24, 1990 and April 29, 1993; Karen Harvey's *America's First City*, Tailored Tours Publications, Inc., Lake Buena Vista, FL, 1992; the *Site of 46 Avenida Menendez* by Sheherzad Navidi of the St. Augustine Historical Society Library, 1993; *The Houses of St. Augustine* by David Nolan, Pineapple Press, 1995; and other historical records of the St. Augustine Historical Society Library. In addition, for each story I tried to interview at least two individuals with personal knowledge of the circumstances.

PREFACE

*I*N SOME CASES I HAVE ALTERED STORIES slightly, changing names, locations, and specific circumstances, in order to protect the privacy of the individuals concerned. In every case I have based my presentations on information received first-hand from individuals I believed to have personal knowledge of the story being presented.

St. Augustine is old; it was one hundred twenty years old when Johann Sebastian Bach and George F. Handel, two of my favorite composers, were born. Its long and colorful history is rich with a unique oral tradition from which these stories were gathered. I hope you enjoy reading them as much as I have enjoyed collecting them into this little book.

*S*T. Augustine is best experienced at night. In the daytime, sights and sounds of a tourist town overwhelm the senses. Throngs of people, bumper-to-bumper traffic, endless rows of restaurants and shops, a constant flow of tour trolleys, raucous music of every variety from bars and stores, and a profusion of attractions all compete for attention. But at night everything is closed. Few people are about. The tour buses and trolleys have stopped running. The stores and restaurants have shut their doors. At night darkness and quiet descend; the sixth sense takes over. At night you can feel St. Augustine. The Ancient City wraps itself around you like a blanket.

Walking the streets of America's oldest city after dark is like stepping through a time warp. In the quiet and the dark, you can smell the sweat of Spanish horses, the aroma of garlic and olive oil wafting from the kitchens. You can hear laughter and soft voices speaking in foreign tongues. Walking these streets at night can be eerie, even spooky. Stopping in front of one of the old houses on Bridge or St. Francis Streets or anywhere in the city, you can feel its age. Sometimes, you can feel something else, too. You may be enveloped by a sudden warmth which is replaced by bone-chilling cold. Or maybe you feel a presence standing next to you, even when you are alone.

Living less than two hours away, I had been in St. Augustine many times before. In fact, my wife and I sometimes drove over just for dinner. But then I had come as a tourist. Now I was here searching for ghosts. I walked slowly down St. George Street in the dark, soaking in the history. Like most of the streets south of the Plaza, St. George Street is not well lighted. The block I was now in was particularly dark. About halfway down the block I stopped in front of an old Victorian house. The house was obviously uninhabited. The bushes and plants in the front garden grew wild and reached out over the rusty wrought-iron fence that surrounded the place. Debris littered the walk—dead branches and leaves, small rocks, and dirt washed onto the concrete by the rain. The porch across the entire front of the house was also covered with leaves and branches. The two large windows on either side of the front door were not boarded up, and some of the panes were cracked and broken.

Rain had fallen earlier, and the dampness enhanced the smell of age and decay. The broken filigree along the eaves, the peeling paint, and the rose vines casting their tentacles across the front and sides completed the ghostly picture.

I stopped in front of the gate and stared up at the haunting structure. I stood on the walk for a long time, unable to move, mesmerized by the scene. I looked up at the second-story windows. There were three of them across the front above the porch. Shredded curtains hung from each one.

Suddenly, I saw movement in the far left window. Something or someone moved the curtains. A shiver ran down my spine. My heart leaped into my throat. I continued staring at the window, not thirty feet away. Then the curtains parted slightly. Yes, I saw movement. The curtains did move. I strained to see better. Was there someone there? Who moved the curtains? Was it a rat? I couldn't tell, but something had moved them. Then I had the strangest sensation. I was enveloped by a numbing cold. Suddenly, I knew that I was not alone. I stood in front of the gate for several minutes. I realized that I was sweating, even on this cold December night. Finally, I gained control of myself, took a few deep breaths, and hurried back up the street toward the Plaza and my hotel.

The next morning I called my friend, Sandy Craig of Tour St. Augustine, to make a reservation for her popular ghost tour, "A Ghostly Experience." Sandy and Karen Harvey of the *St. Augustine Record* are the two foremost authorities on St. Augustine ghosts, and I planned to spend time with each of them. During my conversation with Sandy, I told her about my experience of the previous evening. I could almost see her smiling over the phone.

That evening I met Sandy and the rest of the group at the Old City Gates. After some preliminary conversation and introductions, Sandy led us over to the Huguenot Cemetery, the first stop on the tour. As we walked along, I found myself next to a woman. We introduced ourselves, and I told her I was a writer doing a book on the ghosts of St. Augustine. I discovered that she was a local psychic.

Finally, we arrived at the rear of the cemetery, and Sandy began her gruesome story. She held us spellbound. As she talked, the psychic tugged at my sleeve. When I looked over at her, she simply put a finger to her lips, signaling silence, then redirected her gaze to a tree off to our right in the cemetery. I followed her eyes, but I saw nothing. I looked at her questioningly. Again, she pointed with her eyes to the tree. Still, I could see nothing.

After we left the cemetery for our next stop, she asked, "Didn't you see him?"

"See who?"

"The man in the tree."

"Man in the tree?" I asked with raised eyebrows. "No. No, I didn't."

"Well, don't worry. I'm sure you'll get another chance." Her look and her tone of voice were reassuring.

The tour continued without further incident, for which I was thankful. Sandy's stories were quite chilling in their own right.

After the tour, as the group was breaking up, I invited my new-found friend to go with me to pay a visit to the house on St. George Street. I wanted to find out if I had imagined the whole thing or if I really had seen something. She eagerly accepted, and we strode off into the night. As we walked, I related the events of the night before.

We both fell silent as we approached the house. It looked even more ghostly and terrifying than it had the previous evening. Standing in front of the gate, I searched the windows for a glimpse of whatever I had seen the night before. Now I saw nothing. I pushed open the gate, which squealed loudly as it swung inward. I didn't want to trespass on private property, even if the dwelling were unoccupied, but I at least wanted to get up on the porch. We moved forward.

Slowly we continued. Two paces. Three paces. Four. Five. Six. We reached the bottom step. Cautiously, we climbed one step at a time, feeling for rotten wood in the dark. The stairs creaked eerily with each footfall. Before we realized it, we stood at the front door. We stopped, and the psychic stood quietly for a few moments with her eyes closed. Then she looked at me. "Yes, there is a presence here. She is a young woman who lived here in the 1880s or '90s and died in the house under mysterious circumstances."

We stared at each other a moment, then looked back at the

door. I took a deep breath and exhaled. My heart was pounding. I reached out slowly, put my hand on the doorknob, and twisted it.

The door was locked.

We stood, still and silent, for several minutes. Then, once again, I was surrounded by a bone-chilling cold. Without saying anything, my friend wrapped her arms around herself, indicating she also could feel the cold. Finally, we turned and went back out to the street, closing the gate behind us. As we walked back up the street into the light of the Plaza, adrenaline quickly drained from my system. I laughed out loud.

That was the first such experience I'd ever had, and I hoped it wouldn't be my last.

"Don't worry," my psychic friend said. "If you hang around here very long, I'm sure you'll have as many thrills as you can handle."

THE GALLANT

ON A WARM FRIDAY EVENING in midsummer of 1981, Pat and Maggie Patterson drove up to 214 St. George Street and parked their car. They were both excited, since they had just "closed" on their dream house, one of the oldest—perhaps the oldest—and certainly one of the nicest homes in St. Augustine.

The house was built during the First Spanish Period (1565 – 1763), probably in the early 1630s, although records are incomplete and no one knows for sure. What is certain is that it was the home of Don Pedro Benedit de Horruytinér, the Spanish Governor of Florida from 1646 to 1648 and again from 1651 to 1654. It was built and occupied previously by his uncle, Don Luis de Horruytinér, who was appointed governor in 1633 and served for several years before returning to Spain.

Don Pedro had come to St. Augustine as a young man with his uncle, and had stayed to become a prominent and successful businessman, military commander, and community leader as well as the governor. He died here in 1684, leaving his wife, eleven children, and many grandchildren. Although his name has long since died out, his blood still runs thick in St. Augustine.

Now, after having passed through so many hands and after all these hundreds of years, his house belonged to the Pattersons. In the gathering darkness, Pat and Maggie stood at the front door absorbing the aura of this place, the thick coquina blocks with which the house had been built, the ancient tabby wall around the garden in back, the heavy wooden balcony above them put into place long before this country became a nation. They smiled at each other as they stood there. Maggie was a woman who knew what she wanted, and she had long wanted this house. Pat's great joy was to indulge her. The antiquity of the house almost overwhelmed them, and, of course, there were the ghosts. Pat and Maggie were well aware of the history of the place and knew about the ghosts. In fact, both looked forward to living with the nearly two hundred souls from the past that purportedly occupied the site.

"Well, if there are ghosts in here," Maggie called out in her gentle, but matter-of-fact, voice (for she is also a lady with a presence), "I wish they'd give us a sign!" At that moment all the lights in the house mysteriously came on.

Pat unlocked the door, and the two went inside. There was no one in the empty hallway or living room. They walked through the other rooms downstairs. No one was there. Then they went upstairs. The second floor was completely empty. There was nothing and no one. Finally, they went up to the third floor, which was unfinished. It had been added probably sometime after 1763 and apparently had never been used very much, except by Dr. Horace Lindsley, who bought the house in 1896. Behind the house, next to the old tabby wall along the street, Dr. Lindsley had built a small structure, which he used for his office. Here on the third floor he stored coffins; one of them was still here. Funny, the Lindsley family had owned this house until 1977 and had left that coffin up here all these years. Perhaps it was just too bulky to remove, so no one had bothered. Now there was nothing else here but the coffin.

Pat and Maggie stood there for a few moments, spines tingling, savoring their own thoughts of what might have taken place up here. Then they started back downstairs, turning off lights as they went.

At the bottom of the stairs they turned to go into the kitchen and switch off the lights there. Then they went into the dining room. As they entered the room, Maggie happened to look out the window that faced into the back garden. She caught her breath. "Pat, look!" There in the window was a man, dressed in a soldier's blue uniform, a uniform from the seventeenth century. Was it a Spanish soldier assigned to guard the governor's house? Maggie smiled. The sentry smiled back, saluted, and disappeared into thin air. Pat and Maggie looked at each other and burst out laughing. In the coming years they would see this sentry many times, and his presence would be comforting. After all, who would attempt to rob a house guarded by a ghost?

The following week Pat and Maggie moved into the house. Until recent times the kitchen had been located in a separate building on the west side of the house. This arrangement was common throughout the South until the advent of air conditioning. It kept the unbearable heat of the cooking fires out of the house in the summer. It made the kitchen a little cooler with four outside walls, usually all with windows. And, in case of fire, only the kitchen burned down and not the whole house. On the west side near the kitchen there was a large pantry with an outside door. Food was prepared in the kitchen, brought to the pantry, then served in the dining room next to it. This pantry was Pat's office temporarily. Although the house had recently been restored, there was still some work to be done, and Pat, with his artist's eye, was sitting in his office sketching ideas.

He happened to look out into the dining room, and there sat a large, plump calico cat contentedly staring at him. Pat frowned. His first thought was to yell at Maggie to come get the cat and take it back to the kitchen where the other two Patterson cats stayed, for they were not allowed in any other part of the house. Then he realized that they didn't have a calico cat. "Damn," he said to no one in particular, "I've left a door open," but the outside door was closed. He got up from his chair and walked into the living room and hall. Both the loggia door off the living room and the front door were closed. "Where could it have gotten in?" he asked out loud as he went back into the dining room to get the cat, which still sat resting on the floor in a patch of sunlight. As he bent down to pick the cat up, it disappeared into thin air.

Like the Spanish sentry this cat has also reappeared often throughout the years the Pattersons have lived in the house. In fact, not so long ago, when their two youngest grandsons were visiting, the boys had an experience with the cat. They had been in the kitchen with their grandmother and wanted to go upstairs to watch television. "Don't let the cats out, boys," Maggie yelled after them as they charged out of the kitchen and down the hall. Halfway up the stairs a calico cat suddenly appeared and started downstairs. Both boys felt it brush their legs as it passed. They looked at each other and frowned. "Oh, oh," Zack said, "a cat got out. Gramma's gonna be mad."

Josh thought for a moment. "Hey, wait a minute. Gramma doesn't have a calico cat."

Both boys raced back to the kitchen. "Gramma! Gramma! There's a calico cat on the stairs."

Maggie looked at them and smiled, "Never mind, boys. That's Grampa's Spanish cat." The two shrugged and went back upstairs. The cat was gone.

One Friday evening, sometime later, the Pattersons were preparing to go out. Maggie went to her jewelry box to get a ring. She noticed that three of her nicest were not there. "Pat, have you seen my rings?"

"No, dear. I haven't been in your jewelry box," Pat answered patiently.

This was exasperating, Maggie thought. Her jewelry was either on her person or in her jewelry box. She was very meticulous about that. She tried to think when she had worn any of the rings. It had been months. Rats! Then she thought of her purses. Very improbable. Maggie was as meticulous with her purses as with her jewelry. She had a routine that never changed.

Maggie had a mania for purses. She had hundreds of them, and she selected a purse with the same care and thought that she gave to her dress and jewelry. Maggie was very particular. She never, never carried the same purse twice in a row. When she returned from being out, she always emptied her purse, put the contents on her dresser, and put the purse away in her closet. Then, when she went out again, she chose a new purse.

No, she could not have left the rings in a purse. Still, it was worth checking. But after looking into thirty or forty purses that she might have used in the past few months, she realized the rings could not have been left in any of them. She was very upset, but she went on with the evening, choosing other jewelry, and the rings slipped to the back of her mind.

A year later Pat was gently chiding Maggie about her purses.

"Maggie, do you suppose we could get rid of a few purses? The closet is getting crowded."

Maggie took the hint and began sorting through them to pick out those she would keep. In the back of the closet were several boxes of purses she hadn't used in months, even years, and as she went through these, she opened one for no particular reason. There in the bottom of that purse were her three lost rings.

On another occasion Pat had been given an antique ring by the widow of a close friend. They had been friends for many years, so, besides the ring's value as an antique, it was sentimentally priceless to Pat. Pat never wore the ring but kept it in his jewelry box and took it out only occasionally just to look at it. One day he looked for it, only to find it wasn't there. "Maggie, have you seen my antique ring?" he called to his wife.

"Why, no, dear. I haven't been near your jewelry box."

They searched the dresser, the rest of the bedroom, the bathroom, dressing room, and closet, then the whole second floor. The ring was gone. Pat was beside himself. For many weeks after, he was depressed about losing that ring, because it had meant so much to him.

Then one night about six months later, Maggie had a dream. In the dream a ghostly figure told her about a hidden compartment in the closet wall and told her how to get into it. "You will find something in there," the figure had said.

In the morning she woke Pat up. "You're not going to believe this, dear, but I had a crazy dream last night."

Pat opened his eyes and smiled. "Tell me. I can believe anything, my love."

Then she related the dream. They got up and went into the

closet. Following the instructions the ghost in the dream had given her, they found the compartment. It was too narrow and too deep to see into, so Maggie reached her hand down into it. As her fingers touched the bottom of the compartment they felt something. She grasped it and took it out. Pat's lost ring!

One Sunday morning Pat rose before Maggie to go to early service at the church across the street. He let her sleep because they had been out late the evening before having dinner with friends. He dressed quietly without waking her and left the house.

Sometime later Maggie awoke to a cacophonous racket. It sounded like someone sliding a heavy piece of furniture back and forth across the floor. It was coming from the third floor. "What is Pat doing up there?" she said aloud, angrily. Throwing off the covers, she put on a dressing gown and started for the door. Just then Pat came in.

"What's going on up there?" she barked at him.

Pat had a blank look on his face. "What are you talking about? I've just come in from church."

"Listen," Maggie said.

Pat could hear the noise, too. They went upstairs to the third floor, which was empty except for Dr. Lindsley's pine-wood coffin. The coffin was sliding back and forth slowly across the floor. No one was there. Maggie and Pat shrugged at each other and went downstairs for breakfast. Their ghosts were at work again.

On another Friday evening, the Pattersons invited friends in for coffee. Their guests were Mrs. Maguire, an elderly lady who lived down the street, their friend, Barbara, and her twelve-year old daughter,

Sara. Everyone was sitting around the living room talking when Maggie stopped in mid-sentence and gazed intently into the hall-way. They all turned to see what she was looking at. A tall figure dressed in a cape or raincoat had stepped into the room. His clothes were dark, colorless, and they couldn't quite make out the features of his face. He took two steps into the room, stopped, and looked around as though he had been surprised by their presence. Then he backed into the hall, walked into the living room again, stood for several seconds, and vanished.

The five sat speechless, until Pat broke the spell. "I guess he wasn't dressed for the occasion. At least, he could have excused himself." They all laughed.

The months and years passed, and the Pattersons settled in. Glasses and jewelry and books disappeared, but they always turned up, eventually. The dishwasher in the kitchen had a habit of starting up at odd times, though an electrician and a repairman could find no reason, but the oral threat of pulling the plug always turned it off. At one point, their heavy statue of St. Francis on the loggia began walking toward the garden gate and had to be muscled back to his spot every day. Finally, they moved him into the dining room, and he quit his wandering. But these were minor inconveniences, and the Pattersons got along quite well with their guests. Or was it the other way around?

Still, Maggie longed for a really "significant" experience. She wanted to "meet" someone from the past. Finally, she got her chance. On yet another Friday evening she and her oldest grandson were sitting in the dining room; Pat was in his pantry office next to it. Their grandson was reading, and Maggie was absorbed in study. She and Pat have a passion for Mayan culture and history, and she was taking a course at nearby Flagler College.

Suddenly, the boy looked up. "Grandma, I don't like what they're doing out there."

Maggie was engrossed in her study and wasn't paying much attention. "It's just the cars passing by on the street," she said, and went back to her book.

"No, Grandma, I don't like what they're doing." And, much agitated, he jumped up and ran out of the room.

Maggie looked into the living room and caught her breath. There, walking into the dining room not three steps away was a tall, handsome gentleman dressed in European fashion from the mid-1600s and wearing high cavalier boots and a plumed hat. His clothes were dark shades of gray and black, and he looked like he had just stepped out of a black-and-white movie. There were no sounds of footsteps or rustling of clothes or breathing. The "gentleman" glided toward Maggie and stopped in front of her. Then he smiled, doffed his hat, and bowed gallantly in greeting. Maggie stood and turned toward the pantry to call Pat. When she turned back again, the "gentleman" had vanished.

Several weeks later Maggie received a box of things the previous owner had dropped off, memorabilia and historical items concerning the house. With her busy schedule she didn't get to it for months. Finally, she opened the box and slowly unpacked it. There were historical articles, some small items recovered from an old kitchen in the back, and a couple of French officer's shirt buttons, found in a hidden vault during restoration. But, in the bottom of the box was a picture of a man dressed exactly in 17th Century clothing. The picture was a modern photograph of an actor dressed as Don Pedro Horruytinér, the governor, but his clothes were exactly the same clothes her visitor had been wearing. Had she actually received a visit from the governor himself?

Don Pedro has not called since that time, and the Pattersons have had to be content with their poltergeists, Spanish sentry, and cat. Still, Maggie hopes he will call again. She has many questions she wants to ask, and, besides, it's always flattering to receive the attentions of such a handsome gentleman.

A few weeks before this book went to print, my friend, Sandy Craig, called. She was excited. The Patterson house is one of the stops on her nightly "A Ghostly Experience" tour. Her group of about twelve people was standing across the street from the darkened house by the Trinity Episcopal Church, and Sandy had been talking for ten minutes or so.

Suddenly, the outside light came on and quickly went out. Then the foyer light came on for several seconds and went out. Then, the light on the stairs appeared. One of the men on the tour happened to be looking through the transom window above the front door and saw a woman, actually the bottom half of a woman, because the top of the transom blocked his view. He could make out a floor-length, off-white dress with green and yellow flowers. And he could see the bottom of the woman's petticoats and white shoes, because she had lifted her skirt slightly to keep from tripping. The woman ascended the stairs and disappeared from view. Finally, all the second floor lights came on for a few seconds; then the house went dark. Three others ran to the man's side and were able to see the woman also.

The incident caused quite a stir on the tour, because Sandy knew the Pattersons were not at home. There was no one in the house. Was the governor entertaining a lady guest while the Pattersons were out of town? Later, when Sandy related the incident to the Pattersons, Maggie and Pat just looked at each other and smiled.

CATALINA'S

RICK WORLEY IS ONE OF THE owners of Catalina's Gardens now, but in 1988, when the restaurant was the Chart House, he worked there as a manager. One day he was cutting meat in the kitchen when Lynn, one of his employees, came rushing in from the back room.

"Rick, there's a fire back there; there's a fire in the laundry basket."

As Rick puts it: "I rushed back there to see what the problem was. We used to do our own laundry, napkins, table clothes, uniforms, and things. We had a washer and dryer. During the day, the prep cooks would watch the laundry and make sure everything was okay. I couldn't imagine what Lynn was talking about. When I got to the back room, a laundry basket of clean, dry clothes and napkins was smoldering. There were no chemicals back there. There were no cigarettes, nothing hot enough to have caused a spontaneous combustion. There was no way that fire could have started—but there it was. It was really weird."

Nothing like that has happened since, but there have been countless unexplained and unexplainable events in the house at 46 Avenida Menendez.

The house is very old. Existing records take it back to 1800, but the original house was probably built around 1745, when Juana Navarro, a St. Augustine native born in 1729, married Francisco de Porras. Francisco and Juana had nine children. Catalina, probably the youngest or second youngest, was born in 1753. The family lived in the house, on what was then Bay Street, until 1763 when the Spanish relinquished Florida to the British. The de Porras family sailed for Havana on October 28, 1763, never to return—except for Catalina.

Having spent the first ten years of her life in the house, she had a strong attachment to it. About 1770 she married Joseph Xavier Ponce de Leon in Cuba. In 1784 Spain regained possession of Florida, and Catalina returned to St. Augustine with her husband to reclaim her house on Bay Street.

To her dismay her beloved house, which had been unoccupied during the twenty years of British rule, had been seized as property of the Crown and was a storage shed for the pilots who worked in the bay. Joseph and Catalina petitioned Governor Quesada to recover the house, but it was not returned until 1789. Catalina was thirty-six years old, and she died only six years later, so she wasn't able to enjoy the house of her childhood for very long.

The dwelling was destroyed by the great fire of 1887 that swept through much of St. Augustine, but, thanks to a series of sketches done by John Horton in 1840, the house was rebuilt in 1888 on its original foundation to its original Spanish specifications, this time with poured concrete instead of tabby.

The new building was lived in by various people until 1976 when it became the Puerta Verde Restaurant and, in 1985, the Chart House. Few know it better than Rick Worley. Except for a short period away working in another Chart House restaurant, Rick has been at 46 Avenida Menendez since 1985. "I've been here for almost ten years now. I spend eighty to a hundred hours a week here. I know this house, every creak, every draft, every noise. I know it better than my own home, better than anyone else knows it, and I'll tell you, there's something or somebody here. It isn't threatening; it's very friendly. In fact, a lot of the people who work here enjoy having it around. You know, we even have customers who come back time and time again just in the hopes of experiencing the 'ghost.' Most of my people call it Bridget, but I think it's Catalina."

Back in the Chart House days, Rick had contracted with a local family to clean the place every night, some time between closing and opening the next day. On more than one occasion while cleaning the ladies' restroom on the second floor, one of the family, Ann, would see a woman dressed in a long white dress, almost like a wedding dress, out of the corner of her eye. Always, when she looked, the woman would disappear. Once in 1990, Ann saw her walk right through the restroom door.

Many others have had experiences in the house. Once, Mark, who cleans up during the day, approached Rick, "You're going to think I'm crazy, but on the second floor near the ladies' room, I've been smelling this woman's perfume. It's so strong, it almost stinks!"

Rick laughed. Ann and several of the other employees had been making the same observation for years. It was strange; Mark was new, and he'd never heard any of the stories about the ghost.

On another occasion, when the restaurant was still the Chart House, Rick planned to do an inventory. Normally, he started early, very early, at five o'clock or so in the morning. At about five, Ann was sitting in the lounge taking a break, having coffee and blueberry muffins. She heard a patio door opening and thought Rick was coming in for his inventory. She called out, "Rick, what are you doing here so early?" No one answered. She got up and walked across the room to see who was at the patio door. The door was jiggling and she saw the lady in the white dress, a long white dress with what appeared to be a train, again almost like a wedding dress. The lady looked at Ann, then passed through the patio door to the outside. The door, of course, was locked. Ann grabbed her coffee and muffins and went back into the kitchen with everyone else. Rick didn't get there until almost six o'clock.

Activity hasn't been confined to the first and second floors of the house. Back in the Chart House days Rick's office was on the third floor. At the time one of the waitresses, Mary Kate, who was going to school, often stayed late to use the copier or typewriter and to do her school work. One evening, after an inventory, Rick was at his desk absorbed in his calculator. Out of the corner of his eye, he saw a flash of white pass behind him headed for the copier. Naturally he thought it was Mary Kate. He called out to her, "Mary Kate, what are you doing here?" There was no answer. "Mary Kate?" Still no answer. Rick rose from his desk and went back to the copier. There was no one there. He went down to the second and first floors. There was no one anywhere else in the building. It was locked up. Rick went home without bothering to go back to the third floor.

On several occasions lights have come on after everyone has left. Once, Tracy, Rick, and a waiter all left together. Tracy was the last one out and she was just locking the door when she noticed some of the lights on. She knew she had turned everything off. Rick and the waiter both swore they hadn't gone back in any rooms to turn them on. Even stranger, candles have been lit after everyone has left the building, and, strangest of all, Rick's wife, Gloria, has reported the fire in the fireplace spontaneously igniting on more than one occasion after being cold all night and with no ashes which might have contained hot embers.

But the majority of activity centers around the ladies' restroom on the second floor. In addition to Ann's encounters many other people have had breathtaking experiences. Once, two women customers asked to see the manager. When Rick approached the table, one of them asked, "Is this place haunted, by any chance?"

"Well, let me tell you some stories. Why do you ask?"

Then the woman related that she had been in the bathroom and felt a presence, "like someone was watching me, like there was someone else in the restroom. Well, the feeling was so strong, I opened the door a little to see if anyone was out in the hall, and, of course, there wasn't, but the presence was there, and, finally, I got so uncomfortable, I rushed out. I just had to get out of there."

There is a stack of small tissues on the counter in the ladies' restroom. Melissa, one of the waitresses, goes to the restroom every couple of hours to make sure everything is in order and to replenish the tissues and paper, if necessary. She came to Rick with this story. "It was really weird. I went into the ladies' room about four o'clock, and the tissues were scattered haphazardly all over the counter. I didn't think anything about it. I just put them back in a pile and straightened them up. Two hours later, I went back up there, and the tissues were scattered around again—exactly as they had been at four. That's happened to me twice."

Jason, another long-time employee, sees Catalina, or Bridget, all the time. "At the upstairs waiter's station, we have a mirror, and I often see an image of a woman with a white dress on, out of the corner of my eye, but when I look straight at her, she disappears. And I see her a lot going down the hallway on the second floor. And we hear her a lot, too, after hours when it's quiet."

When asked if these experiences were frightening, he just smiles, "No, not really. I mean, I've gotten chills before, but I've never run down the stairs screaming. Actually, I usually see her once or twice a week. When I don't I kind of miss her. She's really a friendly person, er, ah, ghost. The only thing is, I've never seen her face, and I'd really like to do that."

Psychics, too, have had experiences in the house. Once a woman came in by herself for dinner. While ordering her meal, she began talking to the waitress, Linda, and told her she was a psychic. She talked on, telling Linda that the house was haunted. When she finished ordering, she went upstairs to the restroom. Moments later she hurried downstairs and said, "I have to leave. The presence upstairs is just too strong." And she canceled her order and left.

Another time, during one of the many weekend festivals held in St. Augustine, a group of people from Broward County came in for dinner. Shortly after they arrived, one of the women called Rick to the table and started to tell him all about the ghost in the house. Rick thought it was phenomenal that she knew so much. "There's a ghost in this place, isn't there?" she asked Rick. Rick admitted that there was.

"Well, I can tell you all about her. I honestly believe this room here with the fireplace was her bedroom, and I get the feeling that she is very, very restless because she's had a problem with a man. Something happened in her life, and she's restless because of it." Perhaps Catalina never got to move back into her house, or was Joseph seeing another woman?

Catalina is not the only ghost in the house. Several people, both employees and customers, have reported seeing a man dressed in an old-fashioned black suit, perhaps from around the turn of this century. One time a lady customer asked the waitress who the man in the funny black suit on the far side of the room was. The waitress had no idea. She turned around to look, and there was no one there.

Several times he has been seen near the wine case. A waitress once saw him coming down the stairs and kept an eye on him as he walked toward the wine case. She followed him. When she reached the bottom of the stairs, she went around the corner to the wine case. There was no one there, and there was no other exit from the room—except through the wine case.

Stories from the past mention an unidentified man who died in the 1887 fire. And in 1993 Rick was contacted by a girl who was retracing her family tree. She told him her great grandfather had lived in the house. Sometime around the turn of the century the building was empty and in probate, so the family sent him down from Ohio to live in it. He was in poor health, and his doctor thought the Florida climate would be good for him. He died in the house, around midnight, a short time after arriving. Whoever the man is, his presence has been seen many times in the restaurant, although never with Catalina. Perhaps, they are bickering.

"The weird thing is, we changed the name from the Chart House to Catalina's Gardens on May 21, 1993. Since then, there has been a lot less activity, so I've started to think maybe she's happier now. She has her house back, and it has her name on it."

Still, there are encounters, especially on the third floor where people feel as if they're being followed as they go down the hall. And, of course, many people still feel a presence in the ladies' room on the second floor. "Two paranormals were in here recently and told me that we would see more during drastic changes of the weather, especially from summer to winter, and, when I thought about it, I guess that's true. When we have a cold snap, when it's rainy and cold outside, there does seem to be more activity.

"Some people don't believe it, but there's no question. I'd be the first one to say there's definitely a ghost. It's a friendly ghost, or ghosts; it's not someone scaring the hell out of you, but there's something here."

No one seems to mind, least of all Catalina and her nine-teenth-century companion, who seem perfectly content. Employee turnover is low, and some, like Jason, are even eager to make contact. Customers keep coming back, not only for an excellent food and service, but in hopes of "seeing or experiencing something." Besides, the ambiance is out of this world.

LAPHAM

O
N A CORNER OF HYPOLITA STREET there is a bar, or it used to be a bar. Now it's empty, closed up. It's a two-story structure, built during the British period, with the door opening right onto the street. In the rear there is a small courtyard with a patio and wooden decks shaded by trees—a pleasant spot to while away a hot afternoon with a cold beer. Now it's overgrown with weeds, and the decks are falling apart.

The second story used to be living quarters for the occupants and, until a few years ago, was an apartment which the bar owner rented out for a little extra income. It was actually a nice place to live. Because the walls and floor were so substantial, there wasn't much noise from the bar or the street. Being on the corner and above the street, the apartment got a breeze from several directions. But best of all was the balcony that ran the entire length of the building and looked out over the courtyard. It was covered, of course, and the trees in the courtyard were tall enough to provide additional shade and privacy. A stairway led from the street to the balcony on the south end of the building, and at the top of the stairs was a stout, grate-covered screen door, which could be locked for security.

Joanna had just graduated from college and returned home with her roommate, Emily. Both girls had been lucky enough to get good jobs right in town. Joanna was a native; her family had lived in St. Augustine literally for centuries. She knew everyone, so when the apartment on Hypolita Street became available, she learned of it instantly.

The girls went to look at it, and they both fell in love with the place. It had two bedrooms, a large living room, a small bath, and a tiny kitchen. The living room, and the only outside door, opened onto the balcony, with two windows on either side of the door and two on the opposite wall facing the street. There were no washer and dryer, but Joanna's parents lived not far away, so that wasn't a major problem. Although the place was small, it was well-lit and airy, a lovely little apartment. The two young women were excited; it was perfect for them and within easy walking distance of their jobs. Joanna's mother wasn't thrilled about her daughter living over a bar, but Joanna's enthusiasm soon overcame her mother's reluctance, and the following weekend the two girls moved in.

The girls settled in quickly. They didn't have much furniture, nor did they need any. They both were exhilarated with their new freedom and carefree lifestyle. Neither had been completely on her own before, either living at home or in a college dormitory. There were new things to learn on their respective jobs, Joanna at the Lightner, the wonderful museum across from Flagler College, and Emily at the college. And, of course, there was the nightlife.

They soon got to know the bartenders and regulars downstairs in the bar. It was so much fun just to walk down for a beer. And anytime either wanted peace and quiet, they simply walked back upstairs. Evenings on the balcony were idyllic. There was almost always a breeze, and even in the heat of summer it was cool. Joanna and Emily both loved to sit in the dark, enjoying the breezes and listening to the music from below.

One August evening they had stayed on the balcony longer than usual. It was Saturday night; neither had any reason to get up early the next morning, and the day had been especially hot. Finally, about midnight Joanna yawned and got up from the big rocking chair her mother had given her. She said goodnight to Emily, still slouched lazily in the other rocker, and went inside.

A few moments later Emily stretched and rose from her chair to follow Joanna, but first she went down to the other end of the balcony to make sure the door was locked. As she neared the door she thought she heard footsteps on the stairs. She flicked on the light when she got to the screen door and looked down the stairs. There was no one, but she smelled something peculiar. It was the heavy smell of human sweat and garlic. It smelled like a man who hadn't showered in several days and who had eaten Italian food or something similar. Really strange, she thought, then she turned off the light and went inside.

By the next morning Emily had forgotten the incident, but in the evening the two girls were sitting on the balcony again having a late supper of spaghetti and salad, and Emily noticed the same strange smell.

"Joanna, do you smell that?"

"Do I smell what?" Joanna asked.

"That smell, that garlic and sweat smell."

Joanna sniffed. "No, no, I don't smell anything."

Then Emily described the smell and related what had happened the previous evening.

"You've been spending too much time in the sun, Em." And both girls laughed.

Nothing more happened for two or three weeks. Then, one evening while Emily was on the balcony by herself, looking down on the street at the north end, she heard footsteps. Turning around, she saw someone, or at least she thought she saw someone. Rushing inside, she told Joanna that someone was on the balcony. Joanna looked at her, a little alarmed, and both girls went outside. There was no one. The door at the top of the stairs was locked. They started back inside, when, suddenly, they stopped. Both smelled sweat and garlic.

Again, nothing happened for several weeks, but in mid-September Emily returned to the apartment just after dark. Joanna wasn't home yet. Emily unlocked the screen door at the top of the stairs and walked down the balcony to the front door. As she was unlocking it, she smelled the garlic and sweat again and looked back down the balcony. There he stood, a small man, no taller than she was. He was wearing strange-looking clothing, light-colored, knee-length pants, a dark, tunic-like coat with some sort of belt or sash around his shoulder from which hung a sword, a heavy belt around his waist, and a tall, brimless hat. She couldn't make out many of the details because of the dim light, and she didn't stand there trying to figure them out. Terrified, she screamed, ran into the apartment, and locked the door. Then she turned on all the lights and called the police.

By the time Joanna arrived not long after, the police and the bar owner were there and had calmed Emily down somewhat. While the two officers went through the apartment, checking for evidence of forcible entry, Emily related what had happened to Joanna. The police found nothing and soon left.

Emily refused to spend the night in the apartment, so Joanna took her to her mother's. The next day Emily came back, but only to pack her things. Then she moved out for good.

Joanna was angry with Emily at first. As a native of St. Augustine Joanna quickly realized she was dealing with a ghost. Eventually, she forgave Emily for running out on her, but she wasn't going to give up so easily.

For a few days after Emily left, everything was fine. The ghost of the Spanish soldier, for now that was what Joanna believed she was dealing with, did not appear. But a week later she saw him, the same clothes with the tall hat which reminded her of a bishop's miter, only the front peak was rounded and the rear peak much smaller. What alarmed her most was that he was carrying a rifle. She stood, still and silent, looking at the soldier. Then he melted into the darkness.

The next night he came again. This time she saw him looking in the window. Two or three days passed, and he appeared again. Then his visits became more regular, almost every night she saw him in one window or the other on the balcony. It was always the same. He always appeared at the window, peering in, never smiling. Joanna couldn't find another roommate; the story of her ghost had spread quickly, and no one wanted to live with a ghost. Eventually, the soldier's nightly appearances became too unnerving, and Joanna began to find excuses to stay over at her parents' house more and more often. Finally, two weeks before Christmas, Joanna moved out. For all anyone knows, the Spanish soldier is still there, guarding the rundown little apartment.

*T*HE ST. FRANCIS INN, BY MY reckoning, is the oldest inn in St. Augustine. It has been used by weary travelers since 1845 when Anna Dummett started operating it as a boarding house. It was actually built by Gaspar Garcia in 1791, when he received a grant from the Spanish Crown which included the plot of land on which the St. Francis Inn now sits.

The property passed through a succession of hands until 1838, when Colonel Thomas Dummett, a former English Colonel of Marines, bought the house he and his family had rented the previous two years. The Colonel died a year later, and in 1845 his widow conveyed the house to her daughters, Anna and Sarah. Anna began operating the boarding house in that year.

The original structure was a two-story building not much different from the three-story house that stands today. The third floor, originally an attic, was added in 1888 by John Wilson. Miss

Anna boarded her guests in the main house and used what had been slave quarters behind the house as a kitchen. This small cottage is occupied by guests today.

In 1855 the property was conveyed to Anna's brother-in-law, Major William Hardee, later General Hardee, C. S. A. Anna apparently stayed on to run the boarding house, because Major Hardee was soon promoted and transferred to West Point as the Commandant of Cadets. She is listed as the proprietor of the "Dummett House" in brochures as late as 1870, and she probably was still running the place in 1888, when it was sold to John Wilson.

Through the years the inn has known many owners. It has been enlarged and modernized. It still retains its charm, however, and Regina Reynolds who, together with her husband, Stan, now runs the place is as gracious as I'm sure Miss Anna was.

Naturally, a house as old as the St. Francis Inn has its history and its legends. Like many other houses, especially in St. Augustine, it also has a "presence." My wife and I came up one weekend to visit the St. Francis and to see about the ghost. We checked in on Friday afternoon and were cordially welcomed by Mrs. Reynolds.

After we checked in, April, one of Mrs. Reynolds's employees, escorted us up to our suite on the second floor; unfortunately, Room 3A, where most of the activity is, was already taken. Climbing the front staircase was like climbing into a history book. As we ascended, April told us a little about the place and the ghost on the third floor. She also spoke of a black person's hand, just the hand, some had allegedly seen going down the banister. She herself had never seen it.

Our suite was homey with a sitting room, small kitchenette, large bedroom, and equally large bath. Both main rooms had fireplaces. Our rooms overlooked the street and St. Francis Park, and we could see the Llambias House next to it. It was a pleasant suite of rooms.

We didn't take any time to enjoy our surroundings, however. April had agreed to show us Room 3A before the new occupants checked in. The room is cozy with windows on the west and north sides. Like the other rooms in the inn, it is decorated with period furniture.

The legend is that General Hardee's nephew fell in love with one of their black slaves. Under the circumstances, their love was hopeless, impossible, and the nephew killed himself. His grief-stricken lover, whom some have named Lilly, wanders around the third floor, which was an attic then and possibly the scene of their secret rendezvous, searching for her love.

One visitor described seeing a young black girl, dressed in white, going down the hall. Later, just before going to bed, she saw the girl again in Room 3A. The apparition was not disturbing. In fact, the visitor thought it pleasant, almost playful. On another visit by the same guest the dresser light came on at 2 A.M. and went off twenty minutes later. The manager checked the light the following day and could find no electrical short nor any other reason for the light to have come on. That same morning about 6 A.M. the visitor heard a loud thud and got up to find her purse dumped on the floor.

On a third visit this same guest reported the coffee pot turning itself on and off, and she heard moaning periodically through the night. In the morning while taking a shower, the water started getting hotter and hotter in spite of her attempts to regulate it. Finally, she got mad and ordered Lilly to stop playing around. The water cooled instantly.

One woman guest came to stay in Room 3A purposely because she had heard of the unusual occurrences there. However, the next day she checked out. She had been unable to sleep the whole night because she felt that someone was in the room watching her.

Once during a slow period in mid-week, there was only one

couple staying at the inn; they were in Room 3B across the hall. They had gone out to dinner and were returning late. As they got to the top of the stairs, they saw someone in white pass down the hall just ahead of them and go into 3A. The door did not open and close, and they knew they were the only guests that evening.

The employees, too, have had experiences. When April first began working at the inn, she erroneously believed the ghost was on the second floor, and she thought it strange that she'd never felt anything. Then, she had occasion to work on the third floor, and immediately sensed that someone was watching her. She learned only later that most of the unusual activity was on the third floor.

Another one of the girls regularly cleans Room 3A and likes to watch TV while she works. Her favorite station is MTV and one of the first times she cleaned the room, she had it on. She left the room momentarily to get fresh sheets and when she returned the channel had been changed. She doesn't watch MTV anymore. As Regina tells her, "She (the presence) doesn't like MTV!"

None of the stories I heard were particularly threatening, and everyone who has had contact with Lilly has reported a pleasant experience, even though she is sometimes mischievous.

We stayed at the inn that afternoon for an hour or more, talking with Mrs. Reynolds and some of her employees. We were fascinated by the tales. Finally, we had to leave to meet my young psychic friend, Jennifer.

During dinner I related the stories I had just heard to Jennifer, and she was as enthralled as my wife and I had been. After dinner, we invited her over to walk through the halls, to see if she could sense anything. When we got to the inn, we walked up to the third floor. Although she was aware of a presence on the third floor, especially near Room 3A, we were mystified because she could detect nothing on the staircase. I had assumed that the hand which April had told us about had been seen on the front staircase, the only one I was aware of at that point. But, on the third floor Jennifer asked if there were another set of stairs. We walked down the hall in the other direction and found a back staircase, which we quickly descended. As we went down, I saw goose bumps on Jennifer's arms, and she told us that was where the hand had been. In the foyer, I asked Mrs. Reynolds, and she confirmed what Jennifer had just told us: the hand had been seen on the back stairs—the servants' staircase.

KENNY BEESON IS IN HIS SEVENTIES now and spends his days lounging over coffee at T. K.'s on St. George Street, but as a young man he was a hard-working tailor. Among other things, he also later became the mayor of St. Augustine. In 1946 Frank "Kixie" Kixmiller opened up a men's shop at 38 St. George Street across from T. K.'s. The site is now occupied by the East Coast/West Coast, another clothier's, but for some thirty years or so, it was Kixie's Men's Store, and Kenny Beeson was the tailor.

The front of the store was open to customers, and Kenny had his working area in the rear. The large workroom contained a work table, two sewing machines, a podium for customers to stand on while getting fitted, and, later, a television set. A store-room and a bathroom opened off the main area, and there was an outside door in the rear wall. Kenny's workroom was a comfortable, well-lit place, and he spent many hours there, keeping up with all the business.

One evening he was working late by himself. He was sitting at one of the sewing machines, occupied in hemming a customer's trousers when, suddenly, he heard a doorknob turning. He looked up from his work and watched as the knob of the storeroom door turned, and the door slowly opened. He sat motionless, not knowing what to think, for perhaps ten or fifteen seconds. Then he was enveloped by an over-powering smell of flowers which reminded him of a funeral home. It was a sickeningly sweet smell, like cheap perfume. The smell clung to him. It wouldn't go away. He closed the shop and went home. Even at home he could smell the aroma of those flowers, although his wife couldn't detect the odor.

Days and weeks and months passed, and strange events continued to occur with increasing regularity. At first, Kenny was petrified, but he soon became used to his "visitors," even if at times they were a little unnerving. The bathroom and storeroom doors opened and closed, items in the workroom moved from one place to another, and the scent of those funeral flowers continued. And the events didn't always occur at night. Often, a knob would turn and a door would open in the middle of the day, and Kenny would be encompassed by that sweet aroma, an aroma that only Kenny could detect. Neither Kixie nor the seamstress, Dorothy Giddens, could ever smell it.

Late one evening when all was quiet in the shop and on St. George Street, Kenny heard what sounded like soldiers or sailors marching on a wooden floor or perhaps the wooden deck of an old sailing ship, the rhythmic stomp, stomp, stomp of leather heels on wood in a regular cadence. Later, Kixie and others heard the sound too, even out on the street when no one was around. Now there was no wood flooring in Kixie's, nor in any of the other stores and shops along that section of the street, but the distinct sound of men marching on wooden planks could be heard with some frequency for years.

Years later, after Kenny had installed the television in the workroom, he was working late. His friend, Preston Lay, was keeping him company. While Kenny worked, Preston watched a TV program, which, coincidentally, was a documentary on strange and unusual occurrences. Kenny was sewing a collar on a coat, a job which must be done by hand, so he couldn't watch, but he listened, and he and Preston chatted. All of a sudden, the storeroom doorknob turned, and the door opened. The sickeningly sweet aroma of funeral flowers fairly billowed into the room. Preston turned to Kenny and commented on his strong-smelling aftershave. For the first time, someone else had smelled the strange scent.

As they sat there, the bathroom door suddenly swung wide open. That was enough for Preston and for Kenny, who put down his work and prepared to leave. Before departing, however, Kenny got out a small tape recorder he had recently purchased and put on a blank tape. He pressed the record button and left the recorder lying on the table. Then he and Preston locked up, making sure the bathroom and storeroom doors were closed, turned out the lights, and left.

The next day he eagerly entered the shop to listen to the tape. Of course, as he expected, the storeroom and bathroom doors which he had closed were open. Nothing else had been disturbed. He rewound the tape and turned it on. First, there was the sound of their leaving the previous night. He could distinctly hear the closing and locking of the back door, the sound of his and Preston's cars starting up, and their driving away.

Then there was silence, but only for a few seconds. Soon, the stomping of feet began, followed by strange, unearthly guttural sounds, which made his spine tingle just to listen to them. Doors opened and closed, leather heels marched back and forth on wooden decks, something squeaked—not unlike a mouse or rat, something scratched, like a dog scratching on a door, trying to get in. In the background were those unnatural, unintelligible guttural sounds. At the time Kixie had an old ship's bell in the front of the store, and, once or twice, the sound of the ship's bell could be heard, tolling the early watches. Later, when Kixie and Dorothy Giddens arrived, they listened to the tape and were startled by it. His friend, Preston, came down to listen to the tape, too. (Not long after, Preston Lay died of a heart attack.)

The store was open late on Thursdays and Fridays until eight o'clock. Kixie would often leave early, and there were other times, too, during the day when Kenny was in the store alone. Not long after the store had been opened, Kenny installed a buzzer, which was wired to the front door, so that even when he was alone, he could continue working in the back and be alerted when customers came into the store. Kenny had run a wire from the contact on the front door, up through the dropped ceiling, and back to the buzzer in his workroom. This system worked without any problems for many years.

Then, in the early 1970s, a customer entered, and the buzzer didn't work. Kenny checked his system and found that the wire had been cut, up above, in the ceiling. Kenny knew that no one had any reason for climbing up to the ceiling. No one had been up there.

Finally, he'd had enough. He called Monsignor Harold Jordan down the street at the Cathedral and requested that he come right away to perform the Rite of Exorcism. Monsignor was at first reluctant, because he had had no experience with exorcism. He said that he did know a priest in Miami whom he could call, but Kenny insisted. He couldn't wait for a priest to come all the way from Miami; he needed someone right away, so Monsignor came over that evening, armed with his crucifix and Holy Water.

He performed the rite, walking around the entire store, inside and out, and through each of the rooms, including the storeroom and bathroom. He blessed everything and exhorted the unwanted spirits to depart. The strange happenings stopped after that, everything except the smell. To this day when Kenny comes down for his coffee and passes by the store, he frequently smells the sickeningly sweet aroma of funeral flowers.

But that is not the end of the story. Just down the street is the two-story, Lapinsky Building, with stores at ground level and two lovely apartments on the second floor. The owners of Champs of Aviles Restaurant to the south of the plaza on Aviles Street just across from Artillery Lane live in one of the apartments.

A nun, a sister of St. Joseph, used to walk past the restaurant on Aviles and would occasionally stop in for a chat with the owners. Soon they got to know each other well and became good friends. One day the sister came by with a present, a bright red blouse, which had been given to her. Of course, she couldn't wear it, so she gave it to Champs' owner, who, as it happened, didn't feel very comfortable in red either. But she graciously accepted the blouse and took it home, where she hung it in the back of her closet.

Not long after the exorcism at Kixie's, the couple returned home to their apartment in the Lapinsky Building after closing the restaurant to find the red blouse laid out on the bed. The woman smiled at her husband and asked, "Why did you get this blouse out? You know I'm not going to wear it."

"I didn't get it out. I just came in with you." And they both laughed.

Over the next few months they returned home on several

occasions to find the blouse laid out on the bed. One evening they found a book on the bed. The wife asked, "Didn't we both finish this a couple of months ago?"

He agreed that they had.

"Well, then, why did you get it out?"

"Look, I didn't even know where you put that thing. I didn't get it out."

Not long after the book incident, the couple in the next apartment invited them over for coffee one evening. During their conversation, the woman related that she and her husband had both been waking up together at eleven o'clock and again at two thirty for the last several evenings. There didn't seem to be any reason for it. They'd look out in the street and out the door, but they never saw anything. Neither remembered hearing any noises, but at eleven and two thirty, they both simultaneously woke up. The restaurateurs looked at each other. The same thing had been happening to them.

The neighbor went on, "And that's not all. You know, we have a ghost in our apartment."

Again, they looked at each other. No, they didn't know, but they were beginning to piece everything together.

"Yes, we have a ghost, and it's a man. I know it's a man, because he's very fresh. He keeps slapping me on the behind." Her husband laughed.

The couple laughed, too, but when they got home they had a very serious discussion about the blouse and the book and waking up twice every night. They decided they needed to talk to someone about these mysterious happenings, so they called Karen Harvey, an editor for the local newspaper and an authority on the ghosts of St. Augustine.

Karen contacted a psychic, who came to the apartment with a photographer. The psychic, a woman, walked around the whole apartment, stopping in each room and finally going out to the stair-well. In the stairwell, she said, "This is where I feel the strongest presence of your guest. His name is Henry Barnes, and he was a sailor."

They were all still standing in the hallway by the stairs when the psychic suddenly said to the photographer, "Quick, he's right over my head, take a picture." At that very moment, the couple's lit-tle dog jumped up, flattened his ears, and ran to hide in a cage in a corner of another room. At the same time, an icy cold blast of air enveloped them all. The psychic exhorted Henry to leave, but she was unsuccessful.

After the psychic's visit, activity seemed to increase. One night the woman was at her dressing table getting ready for bed. Her hus-band was already asleep. Something caught her eye just outside the open bedroom door. She looked and saw a white, flowing apparition on the stair banister. Then it disappeared.

The next day she called Karen back and was referred to Kenny Beeson. Kenny told her of his experience and suggested she call the monsignor. Monsignor Jordan came over in the afternoon and went through the same exorcism ritual he had done at Kixie's. That was the last anyone has seen or heard of Henry Barnes. Perhaps he returned to the sea, or maybe he's wandering up and down St. George Street.

There are many stories about Flagler College, the former Hotel Ponce de Leon. The extravagant lifestyles of the wealthy guests who stayed in the hotel were fertile ground for myth, legends, and stories: secret subterranean passages; closed chambers in the attic; dark, mysterious rituals in hidden places. Even if most of the tales are untrue, they are delicious fodder for young students who now occupy these halls.

*A*FTER THE RELATIVELY QUIET decade of the 1870s, St. Augustine began a period of unprecedented growth and luxury it had not experienced before and hasn't seen since. In the early 1880s the city began staging a Ponce de Leon Celebration for winter visitors. In attendance in 1884 was a powerful and wealthy tycoon, Henry Flagler, honeymooning with his second wife, Alice. He returned a year later with grandiose plans to develop St. Augustine into the American Riviera for the country's social elite.

Before the turn of the century he had transformed the town and changed it forever. First he filled in Maria Sanchez Creek. Then he built the Hotel Ponce de Leon, which later became Flagler College, followed in quick order by the Alcazar, across King Street from the Ponce de Leon, and the Cordova, facing the garden between the two larger hotels. The Alcazar later became the Lightner Museum and the Cordova became local government offices.

These commercial enterprises were only beginnings. Before he was through he had paved streets, built a baseball field, established a bus line, started a dairy and a laundry for his hotels, built the Memorial Presbyterian and Grace Methodist Churches, donated money and land for the Catholic Cathedral and the Ancient City Baptist Church, and developed a subdivision north of his hotels. The list goes on and on. There was very little that Flagler did not directly touch in St. Augustine in the closing years of the last century.

But his beneficence was not appreciated by everyone in town. Some saw him as a self-aggrandizing bully, a pompous ass. What was good for Henry Flagler was good for St. Augustine. To many, Flagler's renaissance was unwanted. However, his influence was undeniable. And so, it was inevitable that upon his death on May 20, 1913, many stories about the man would flourish. They may or may not be founded in truth, but they are a part of the oral tradition of the city.

Flagler died in Palm Beach and his body was shipped to St. Augustine to lie in state in the rotunda of the Ponce de Leon, then to be buried in the Memorial Presbyterian Church. On May 30, 1913, all the Florida East Coast Railway trains stopped around the state. The funeral cortege gathered in the rotunda of the Ponce de Leon to carry Flagler's body to the Memorial Presbyterian Church for burial. Suddenly, in the hushed silence, the great doors of the rotunda slammed shut, startling and unnerving those present. After a few moments, calm prevailed, the doors were opened, and the entourage escorted the body to the church. Later that day a janitor was cleaning up in the rotunda and happened to look at a peculiar tile in the intricate designs on the rotunda floor. The tile he saw was the size of a thumbnail, and on it was the face of Henry Flagler! He intended to stay in the Ponce de Leon forever. That tile, with Henry's face, remains where it was found to this day.

In 1968 the Ponce de Leon became Flagler College, one of the country's finest small, liberal arts colleges. In the early '80s a young man named Mark came to school here and moved into a room on the third floor of the west wing, not far from the rotunda.

Every day he passed through the rotunda on his way to and from classes and meals. Of course, it wasn't long before he heard the stories about the ghosts that roamed the halls and about Henry Flagler. He didn't believe any of it. But he was curious, and one afternoon, with little else to do, he searched the rotunda for Flagler's tile. He was surprised when he found it.

From then on, laughing, he would always stop at the tile, rub it, and invite Mr. Flagler to come visit him. This went on for several weeks, and Mark was even less inclined to believe in the ghost of Henry Flagler, or any ghosts for that matter.

Then, late one Wednesday afternoon he made his usual stop. While his classmates watched he bent down, rubbed the tile, and invited Henry to his room. "Come on, Henry! Come on up and visit!" The boys laughed, the girls giggled, and they all went their separate ways.

Mark went to his room, crossed it, and threw his books on his desk. While he was facing the desk he sensed someone enter. He wasn't surprised because he had left the door open. "Come on in," he said and turned around. No one was there. He stood still for several seconds, not certain of what was going on. Then the door closed.

"Henry? Henry?" he asked in a less confident voice than he had used in the rotunda. There was silence, but he was surrounded by what he later described as an overpowering presence. Then the door opened, and he was alone again.

He was so shaken by the event he closed the curtains, turned off the light, and left. He has never been back to St. Augustine.

Flagler's second wife, Alice, or Ida Alice as friends called her, was a spunky, extravagant strawberry blonde. Pert, pretty, and lively, she was popular, if sometimes erratic in her behavior. History says she became insane and was institutionalized. Legend says she went crazy from playing with a Ouija board and died in a mental hospital, a raving, violent, mad woman.

In recent years a young coed came to Flagler and moved into the east wing of the main building. She was pretty and perky and looked very much like Ida Alice. Shortly after she arrived, the apparition of a pretty, young strawberry blonde was seen moving around the halls. Soon the ghost settled in the young woman's room.

The presence wasn't malicious, but it was disturbing. In the middle of the night the young woman would wake up with Ida Alice standing before her bed, watching her in stony silence. In the evenings she would return from the library and see the face of Flagler's wife in the door as she opened it. Finally she asked for another room, but even that didn't help. Before the end of the first semester, the girl left Flagler and went to Rollins College in Orlando. Apparently Alice didn't follow her there.

There is also a woman in black who allegedly is still seen on the top floor of the west wing. Supposedly, Flagler had a mistress. At one point Alice came for an extended stay in the Ponce de Leon. Henry was quite unnerved, of course, and fearing the two might meet if he allowed his mistress to wander around, he confined her to a suite of rooms out of the way. Apparently he wasn't willing to send her off while his wife was in town.

The suite was well-appointed, with mirrors on the ceiling and walls and servants always at hand. However, the young woman, who always wore black, needed more excitement. As time went on she became more and more depressed and finally, late one evening, driven to the depths of despair, she hanged herself.

LAPHAM

MANY OF THE STORIES OF GHOSTS in St. Augustine are founded in history. They can be traced to specific people who have died and continue to haunt a particular location. The governor at 214 St. George Street, Catalina at Catalina's Gardens, and the slave in the St. Francis Inn are all examples. There are some ghosts, however, who just evolve. They may be very real, but no trace of them can be found among the living. Any evidence of their previous existence has been lost in history.

One such apparition is the ghost that haunted the Upham Cottage at the south end of town. The magnificent twelve-room Victorian was built by Colonel John Upham in 1892 as a "winter cottage." It was the center of much gaiety and elegant social life during the Flagler period. Colonel Upham and his young wife were among the elite of St. Augustine's winter residents. The colonel died in 1898, but his wife retained ownership of the house until 1915, often renting it to winter visitors from the North.

After Mrs. Upham sold the house it passed through many hands as a private residence and an apartment building. In the 1970s it was restored to its original grandeur and is now one of the most beautiful private homes in St. Augustine. Although it is not open to the public, the house is well-worth passing by and viewing from the street.

In 1979 the Upham Cottage contained several apartments. Ms. Bobbi Bay moved into one of them on the top floor. Her bedroom was spacious and airy with tall windows on two walls. There was a door, locked from the bedroom side, that led to the attic. She had no reason to open it, no reason to go upstairs, so she never bothered.

But from the very first day she moved in, she heard music coming from someplace, though she couldn't figure out exactly where. She soon learned that two teenagers lived downstairs and, perhaps, they were playing the music. However, she thought it a little strange, because the music sounded like a harpsichord. What teenager would be listening to a harpsichord? Still, that seemed to be the only explanation. Also, she noticed the morning following her first night in the house that the attic door was unlatched. In fact, every afternoon when she returned home from work, that door was ajar.

For days the music continued, often late into the night. Finally, after several weeks, Ms. Bay went downstairs and asked the youngsters to please stop playing the harpsichord, especially in the evenings when everyone was home. The two young people insisted that they were not playing harpsichord music; they wouldn't be caught dead. One of them, David, told her that the music actually was coming from a ghost in the attic, a young woman named Claire. A likely story, thought Ms. Bay. She didn't believe them. She didn't believe in ghosts.

But night after night she still heard the music. Young people had no consideration for others it seemed. Exasperated, she decided that she would catch the two in the act. The next evening she heard the harpsichord playing again and hurried downstairs to what had once been Colonel and Mrs. Upham's ballroom. As she entered she stopped, astonished at what she saw. There in the middle of the room stood a pretty, auburn-haired woman in her mid-twenties. She was wearing a gown of yellow satin. "What is going on here?" Ms. Bay asked aloud, knowing that what she was seeing wasn't real. Seconds later, the apparition disappeared into thin air.

Ms. Bay saw "Claire" many times after that, usually passing through the bedroom and heading up to the attic, unlatching the door and leaving it ajar in the process. Once, the ghost actually bumped the bed and woke Ms. Bay. Claire didn't say anything. She just walked across the room, opened the door, and walked up the stairs. After that experience, Ms. Bay left the attic door unlatched.

The presence was not threatening. Ms. Bay never felt uncomfortable or frightened in its presence, but she quickly came to believe in ghosts. In fact, a short time after seeing Claire in the ballroom, Ms. Bay went down to apologize to the two teenagers who lived below. They accepted her apology and laughed. David explained. The ghost was a young woman, the wife of a ship's captain who was often at sea for long periods. Apparently, because she was so young and pretty, he kept her locked in the attic while he was away. Her only entertainment was her harpsichord. She died in the attic while her husband was gone.

The captain and his lovely young wife, Claire, have been lost in history. Perhaps they never existed. Although others who have lived in the house since have reported noises and music coming from the attic, the current owners have not been bothered and only smile patiently when asked about their ghost. Still, Bobbi Bay, who has long since moved, will swear to Claire's existence. She believes in ghosts whether they can be found in history or not!

ICKERSONS'

*J*OHN AND REGINA DICKERSON LIVE on Cincinnati Avenue at the north end of town in a wonderful, old home built around the turn of this century. Built mostly of stone with a stone fence across the front, the house is an imposing structure, very distinctive and unique. The Dickersons have taken great pains to restore it to its original condition. In fact, that is their specialty. They have recently bought an old house in Tennessee which they intend to restore as time and money permit as a retirement home. But for now they are very satisfied with their house on Cincinnati Avenue. They love it.

Neither Mr. nor Mrs. Dickerson believes in ghosts, but not long after they moved in and started renovations "some crazy guy" came to the door and asked Regina if she'd "seen the old lady, yet." The Dickersons were well aware of the stories surrounding the house. They knew that Fred and Lottie Capo, who had built it, had both died there as had several other owners. But, no, she hadn't "seen the old lady, yet," and to this day neither of them have seen anything.

Still, "the neighbors are a little paranoid," as Regina puts it. She thinks some of them let their imaginations wander too far. There are stories about the ghost being afraid of fire, and a recurring legend that the house is going to burn down. One Christmas, Regina had decorated her home with poinsettias throughout the house. A neighbor, one evening, seeing the reflection of the beautiful red flowers in the window and knowing the Dickersons were away for the evening, called the fire department. "We can hardly barbecue or light a fire in the fireplace without someone calling to see if everything is all right, but we don't mind. We have terrific neighbors."

Back in the early '80s, before the Dickersons bought the house, a young man I'll call Mark, who lived in the house at the time, approached a Mr. Barron (not his real name) whom he worked with and asked if he knew anything about ghosts. "No, I don't know anything about ghosts; I don't believe in ghosts." But, Mark persisted and half-convinced Mr. Barron that he lived in a "haunted" house. Mr. Barron, a long-time St. Augustine resident, finally agreed to help Mark find someone who might help.

That evening at home Mr. Barron related the incident to his wife who, coincidentally, earlier that day, had met a psychic. Mr. Barron called the man, and he agreed to come look at the house.

Arrangements were made, and the following Saturday Mark and his girlfriend, and Mr. Barron and the psychic, met at the house. Slowly, the four went through the entire house, stopping often as the psychic focused his attention on this or that. Finally, they went back out on the front porch. "Well, there is a ghost in there," the psychic said, "an older lady who died here. Apparently she was unable to get up the stairs to her bedroom in her later years and was stuck on the first floor. And another thing, too, I get the feeling this place is going to burn down soon."

Later a neighbor came over and told Mr. Barron about the light that many in the neighborhood saw at night. It looked like a candle shining in an upstairs window. The window was in the bedroom that had been the old woman's. Well, Mr. Barron had just been up there and didn't see how anyone could see a light in the window, but he didn't argue. Some people were just a little crazy, he thought. The neighbor went back across the street, and Mr. Barron was left alone, sitting on the porch.

Through the open door he could hear Mark and the others talking upstairs in the bedroom. Then, he heard something else, a door closing and footsteps walking along the upstairs hall. The sound stopped at the head of the stairs, then started again and came downstairs and across the foyer. The screen door opened and closed, the steps came across the porch, something brushed against his leg as it went down the front steps and faded on the concrete walk. Mr. Barron sat there, astonished, not knowing what to think.

Finally, the others came downstairs and outside. Sheepishly, Mr. Barron said to them, "She's not in there anymore; she just left." The psychic smiled, "We know; we heard her leave."

Well, that's the only story the Dickersons have heard about their house. Of course, the house hasn't burned down, and the Dickersons have had no experiences. And what about the bedroom? Mrs. Dickerson laughed. "I keep a light on all night long, and I never go up there at night, but," she quickly added, "guests stay up there all the time, and no one has ever had any problems."

And what about their place in Tennessee? She'd said that several people had died there, and that it sat right next to an old family cemetery with sixty graves in it. "Oh, you couldn't pay me to go in that cemetery at night." She laughed again. "I guess I'm a little superstitious—but I still don't believe in ghosts!"

*J*UST DOWN THE STREET FROM THE Dickersons, Randy and Linda Bruner own an equally attractive home which was built sometime between 1917 and 1924. The area around Cincinnati Avenue is known as the Rhode Tract, named after the man who laid it out and built many of the homes. The Bruner's house, like many of the others along the street, was built for an executive of the Florida East Coast Railway. The railroad's offices were just a few blocks away, down Ponce de Leon Boulevard at One Malaga Street. The Bruners' home was originally owned by John and Alaska Parre; both of their names appear on the original deed, but two years later when the Parres sold the house, Alaska's name was missing. Presumably, she died in the interim.

Unlike the Dickersons, the Bruners do believe in ghosts. They believe Alaska Parre haunts their house. Although Linda has never seen Alaska, Randy has, and he describes her as a very attractive, older woman with long gray hair, wearing a bluish-gray garment. She always seems to float through the rooms, up and down stairs, and often she flicks lights on and off and plays music; she loves Vivaldi. Alaska is a very charming, friendly person, and neither the Bruners nor any of their guests have ever felt threatened.

Once, when a friend came to visit, her seven-year-old had to use the bathroom. Linda pointed the little boy up the stairs and told him where the bathroom was. A few minutes later, the child came running excitedly downstairs, his pants not quite all the way up and still unbuttoned. While he was going to the bathroom, a picture on the wall suddenly floated away, around the room, and back to its place on the wall. Alaska was having a little fun with the boy and was probably laughing at that very minute.

Often, when Linda does the dishes, someone pulls her hair gently back and tucks it behind her ears because her hands are wet and soapy, and she can't do it herself. Sometimes small items are hidden, but they soon show up again, especially when they're hidden too well, and the Bruners can't find them. Alaska loves to have fun, but she is always kind and gentle. The Bruners have two cats, and both are now used to Alaska, although at first, Linda could always tell if Alaska was around because the cats acted so strangely. Now, even when Linda can feel Alaska's presence, the cats just stay curled up. Alaska does tease them a little, however, but in a gentle way.

When the Bruners first moved in and were busy renovating the house, Linda was on a ladder, painting a ceiling in one of the rooms—the ceilings are fourteen feet high—and someone or something tickled her. She looked around and could see nothing. Only one cat was in the room, and it was asleep. She thought it was really strange, because no one else was in the house, and she was ten feet in the air on the ladder. Then she was tickled again. Finally she realized it was Alaska, and she started laughing. The tickling stopped, and Linda could almost feel Alaska laughing, too.

But the most startling thing that ever happened occurred even before that. When the Bruners moved in, there was shag carpet on the stairs, which they immediately decided to replace. Their stairway is a reverse stairway, five steps up to a landing, then seventeen more going up in the opposite direction. The first or second day the Bruners were in the house, Linda was at the top of the stairs, trying to pull the shag carpet free; it wouldn't come loose. She should have been more careful, but she was concentrating on getting the carpet up and wasn't thinking. Facing the top of the stairs, she yanked with all her might, and the carpet broke free. Suddenly, she found herself falling, catapulted down the stairs. Just as suddenly, she felt a force catch her in mid-air and cradle her as she floated down, like a feather, to land softly on the landing without even a thump. She didn't even have any bruises. Of course, it was Alaska. She had saved Linda's life, or at least kept her from very serious injury.

For the Bruners, Alaska is not just a ghost. She is a member of the family and a life-saving angel. They cannot imagine life without her.

LAPHAM

ANCIENT CITY ANTIQUES OCCUPIES 26 Toques Place now, and once it was a restaurant, but before the restaurant, it was a private residence. It was built in 1910 as a carriage house or servants' quarters for a larger estate. When the main house of the estate burned to the ground, the owners moved into the smaller building.

Jennifer was eight years old when her family moved into the house. Strange happenings occurred from the very start. The first incident took place the day they came to look at it, even before they moved in. The family had walked all through the house with the owner, then gathered in the living room. The adults were busy talking, and Jennifer had to go to the bathroom. While she was in the bathroom she happened to look into a full-length mirror on the wall and saw "squiggly lines." She couldn't figure it out, but when she moved her leg, the lines reflected onto it, and they read "hi" in cursive writing. At eight she couldn't read cursive very well, but she did know "hi."

She went downstairs and told her sister, "The mirror in the bathroom said hello to me."

Her sister, Stephanie, who was three years older, frowned. "That's stupid; you're crazy."

"No, Stephanie, it said, 'hello,'" Jennifer insisted and pulled Stephanie upstairs to show her. There was nothing there, nothing on the mirror. Jennifer swore that she had seen a reflection on her leg, a reflection from the mirror.

"Look, Jennifer, if 'hi' was reflected on your leg, it would have to look like this (and she drew the word backwards in the air with her finger), but there's nothing there. There is no way you could have seen that." And she stomped downstairs in disgust to get their mother.

"You saw what?"

"Mother, the mirror said 'hi' to me, in cursive on my leg."

"Oh, Jennifer, you couldn't have seen anything. There's nothing in the mirror. There's nothing around here in this bathroom that could have reflected 'hi' in the mirror." No one would believe Jennifer.

And so, the family moved in. The three children, Stephanie, Jennifer, and John, their nine-year-old brother, had rooms upstairs, and the mother, Sara, a room on the first floor. Jennifer had a front room. Large and spacious with a closet all along the back wall, it probably had been the master bedroom. There were windows on the north side and on the front, west side overlooking the porch. Jennifer loved it and quickly had her many stuffed animals arranged around the room with her two favorite bears, Furry and Shy, who were inseparable, in the middle of her pillows. Jennifer was very organized for an eight-year old.

The family also had pets, two large dogs, an Airedale named Dana, and Freda, a Lab. Both dogs were extremely intelligent. They could raise windows, lift latches on screen doors, and even turn knobs to open bathroom and bedroom doors. And yet, they were very well trained and obedient. Both were housebroken and mannerly. Even though they were big dogs, they never caused any problems in the house.

However, soon after moving in, the family went out for a couple of hours and left the dogs in Jennifer's room. When they returned, the room was in shambles. The bedspread had been ripped from the bed, the pillows shredded, the curtains torn down, and clothes and stuffed animals scattered everywhere. And both dogs had had accidents on the carpet. Something had badly frightened them. Curiously, they hadn't opened the door and just left the room, which both were capable of doing. The next time the family went out, the dogs were left in Stephanie's room, and there was no problem.

There were other aggravations. Jennifer's closet was divided into sections. The section next to the outside wall apparently had been built for shoes because it was filled with racks and a high shelf which probably had been used to store shoe boxes. Not long after Jennifer was settled in her room, Shy, one of her two favorite teddy bears, disappeared. She ran crying to her mother. At first, Sara thought Stephanie or John had hid the stuffed animal; neither was above teasing their little sister. She scolded them, but neither would admit to the prank, so she went up to search Jennifer's room thoroughly. She found Shy in the closet on the back of the shelf above the shoe racks.

Two days later Shy disappeared again. Again, Sara scolded Stephanie and John and, this time, sent them to their rooms. Once again, she found Shy on the shelf in the closet, in fact, in exactly the same spot as before.

A week later, neither of the older children were around; Stephanie was with friends, and John was outside playing. Shy disappeared yet again. This time Sara went directly to the closet to find him, and, sure enough, he was up in his accustomed spot on the shelf. After that, Shy disappeared with regularity all the years they lived in the house, and Jennifer soon learned to climb on a chair and retrieve her wandering teddy bear herself.

Once, Sara's friend, Nancy, came to visit and stayed in a room downstairs. Late one evening after everyone was asleep, Nancy came in and woke Sara; she said she heard John crying for his mother. Sara got up, put on a robe, and went upstairs. John was sound asleep. Sara went back down and got in bed. A short time later Nancy came in again. She could hear John crying, "Mommy, mommy, mommy!" Again, Sara went up and found John sleeping soundly. A third time Nancy came rushing in. "Sara, John is sitting at the top of the stairs and calling you."

Sara was angry now. "Look, Nancy, he is nine years old. He doesn't cry for me anymore. He hasn't cried in the middle of the night for years."

"Sara, I can see him sitting at the top of the steps." Nancy was standing in the doorway of Sara's room.

"He can't be!"

"Well, he is."

Before Sara could get to the doorway to look, the boy Nancy had seen disappeared. They went upstairs together and into John's room. They found him sleeping soundly and wrapped in his blankets, like a cocoon. It was obvious that he hadn't been awake.

On another occasion, Sara's friend, Shirley, came to stay with the children while Sara went to visit relatives in Jacksonville. The children were very self-sufficient, very independent. Stephanie at eleven was an excellent cook, and, together, the kids could take care of themselves. Shirley expected to be no more than an adult presence in the house while Sara was gone.

The second night she was there she had a dream, a very real dream, it later seemed to her. In the dream, a small boy came into her room and woke her up. He was a nice little boy, very polite, and he wanted to show her his room. "Come upstairs and see my room. You must see my room." He took her by the hand and led her up the stairs. Halfway up, she stopped.

"What's wrong?" he asked.

She hesitated. "Why, I don't know. I . . . "

"Come on," he smiled up at her and pulled her up the stairs.

As they reached the top of the stairs he looked at her with an impish grin and said, "I'm dead, you know." With that she woke with a start and broke into a cold sweat. The two dogs were on either side of her. Freda was snapping at something above her head. Horrified, Shirley jumped out of bed, packed her bag, and left the house, leaving a note behind for Sara. "Next time you leave, take your spirits with you!" Shirley never visited again.

Several months later Sara went out, and two teenage girls came to sit with the children. Jennifer and her friend, Stacy, were in Jennifer's room playing. Suddenly, they heard a child's voice crying out, "Help me! Help me!" They looked around and could see no one. John was not outside the door trying to scare them. They walked all around the room trying to find the source of the voice. They ended up at the window, and the sound seemed to be coming from just outside. Excited, they rushed downstairs for the sitters, and all four girls returned. They stood in the middle of the room and listened. "Help me! Help me!" the small voice cried out again. The sound came from a front window sill. It sounded like a little boy calling to his mother. The two teenage sitters couldn't hear the voice, but Stacy heard it and Jennifer heard it. Immediately, all four girls were seized with terror and raced downstairs. They stayed together in the living room until Sara got home. Stephanie and Jennifer slept with Sara that night.

Unusual incidents continued to occur in the house, especially with Jennifer. Periodically, she felt the presence of someone in her room, and often she heard noises that no one could identify. Shy disappeared with regularity, always to be found in the closet. And wind would loudly rush through the attic. Finally, Sara decided to move.

Another strange thing happened as they prepared to leave the house. Sara decided to have a yard sale and set everything up out front. As the morning progressed, Jennifer and her friend, Stacy, watched with detachment from the top of the stairs inside the house. About mid-morning a woman came with a little girl perhaps a couple of years younger than Jennifer. She was into everything. She whined. She was impolite. She was very sassy to her mother. She was obviously spoiled, and not a very nice child. Jennifer and Stacy watched, neither of them liking this little girl. Eventually, the child came into the house and went up to use the bathroom. When she came back out, she stopped on the steps and pestered the two girls, who scolded her. In a huff she plopped down on the step above Stacy, who was sitting on the step above Jennifer. All of sudden, the girl lurched forward against Stacy who fell against Jennifer. Jennifer turned to see what had happened. Stacy turned to glare at the little girl. The girl turned around to see who had pushed her. No one was there. She screamed and raced out of the house in fright.

After everything had been moved out and the family had found a new home, Sara and the children returned to clean the house. Jennifer noticed a red sap oozing from the banister at the top of the stairs. Her mother told her, "The banister's bleeding; your ghost misses you." In later years Jennifer heard another explanation.

Supposedly, there originally had been a wall where the banister was located. The wall often oozed what looked like blood. Some say it was the blood of the little boy's grandmother, who allegedly died a violent death in the house. Several times the wall was covered over, but it continued to ooze bloody-looking fluid. Finally, the wall was replaced with the railing. No one has ever confirmed this version, but that is the legend.

Jennifer has been back to the house many times since her family moved out and has talked to the various owners. One of the owners reported seeing a woman wearing a long skirt walking downstairs. He also had problems with doors locking and unlocking. In fact, after several experiences, he finally had the house blessed by a priest.

Subsequent owners have had no problems. Perhaps the little boy and his mother or grandmother finally found each other and are at peace.

On St. George Street, midway between the Cathedral and the gates, the Pellicer-de Burgo House now stands, constructed by the Historic St. Augustine Preservation Board in 1974. The Paffe Stationery Store used to occupy the site at 49 St. George Street. The building actually included three addresses: 49 St. George was the stationery store and print shop owned by the Paffes; 51 St. George was the address of the apartment upstairs, which ran the length of the building and was occupied by the Paffes; and 53 St. George, a toy store and card shop. The entire building was owned by the Paffe family.

In late September of 1927 a hurricane raged along the coast. Seventy-mile-per-hour winds drove torrential rain and debris horizontally down St. George Street. Streets were flooded. Power was out. Windows were closed and shuttered. Doors were bolted. Still, the rain seeped in through microscopic openings and added to the already high humidity. No one dared venture outside, except in dire emergencies.

Two days before, Nurse Maggie Hunter had stopped by to check on Mrs. Paffe, who was ill and bed-ridden. Her condition seemed serious to Nurse Hunter. She decided to stay and sent word back to the hospital.

Now it was evening of the third day. The hurricane had raged for two days, and Mrs. Paffe's condition had improved little in that time. Maggie went to the kitchen to warm some milk for her patient; Mrs. Paffe could keep little else down. When the milk was heated, she took the pan off the stove, poured the warm liquid into a glass, and started down the hall, passing by the study where Mrs. Paffe's son, Clement, sat bent over his ham radio, passing and receiving information about the hurricane.

As Maggie stepped into Mrs. Paffe's bedroom, she saw, kneeling beside the bed, the shadowy form of a nun, wearing the habit of the Sisters of St. Joseph. She could not see the nun's face, but she could clearly see her hands moving swiftly over the beads of her rosary, obviously praying for Mrs. Paffe. Maggie had been in the house for three days and knew that no one had entered or left in that time. She was quite shaken and rushed back to the study to tell Mrs. Paffe's son.

He acknowledged Maggie and was quite unconcerned. "Oh," he shrugged. "That's just Sister Mary Helen. She always shows up when anything serious happens." And he went back to his radio. When Maggie went back to Mrs. Paffe's room, the nun was gone, and Mrs. Paffe was feeling much better.

That afternoon the weather improved, and Maggie returned to her own home. Mid-morning, three days later, Maggie stopped by the Paffe home to check on Mrs. Paffe. Her son answered the door and Maggie inquired after the elder woman. He was concerned.

"She's been babbling about a Spanish sentry coming to take her home. Except for that, she's about the same as she was."

Maggie entered the house and headed toward Mrs. Paffe's bedroom; the son went down the hall to the kitchen. As Maggie entered, she froze. There, standing by Mrs. Paffe's bed, was what appeared to be a blue-coated, seventeenth-century Spanish sentry. She turned and rushed back down the hall, calling for Mrs. Paffe's son. Together they returned quickly to the old woman's room. The Spanish sentry was gone, and Mrs. Paffe lay lifeless with a peaceful countenance.

THE CASABLANCA

*T*HE CASABLANCA INN AT 24 Avenida Menendez is one of St. Augustine's most elegant bed and breakfasts. It was built in 1914 in the Mediterranean Revival style and recently renovated to its original grandeur. With its elegant rooms and sweeping view of the Matanzas Bay, it is a wonderful place to stay and is very popular with visitors.

In 1919 Congress passed the Prohibition Act prohibiting the manufacture and sale of alcohol in the United States. A thriving black market soon evolved. Treasury agents across the nation were hard-pressed, in fact, were unable to keep up with all the illegal activity that surrounded the trade. St. Augustine became an important center for smuggling booze into the country from Jamaica, Puerto Rico, Cuba, and other islands in the Caribbean. Although there was real risk in smuggling, only a handful of agents were assigned to the Florida coast from Jacksonville to Mosquito Inlet, now Sebastian Inlet, below Daytona Beach, so the odds were heavily in favor of the rum runners. Still, they were careful and didn't take any needless chances.

During the 1920s and '30s, the Casablanca was owned by an elderly lady who ran it as a boarding house. She kept a clean, inexpensive, and comfortable place and served excellent food, and lots of it. So, her boarding house was popular with traveling salesmen—and Treasury agents, who were usually on a tight budget. Because it was so popular, the agents, and everyone else who wanted to stay there, had to call ahead to make reservations. Therefore, the old lady was able to keep pretty close track of the Treasury agents, at least when they were in St. Augustine. This was valuable information, and she was well aware of that fact.

Soon, she was able to parlay this knowledge into a very profitable business. Smugglers would sail up the coast at night and heave-to a couple of miles offshore. Because of the location of her boarding house on the bay, a light from the top of the building could be seen for many miles at sea. If the coast was clear, if there were no agents in town, the old lady would go up to her widow's walk with a lantern and swing it back and forth. The rum runners knew, then, that they could come into port, and they would rush in, speedily off-load their illicit cargo, pay the old lady, and race back out to sea.

Finally, in 1933 Congress repealed prohibition, but not before the old lady become a millionaire. Eventually, she died and was buried in the Huguenot Cemetery, but her light can still be seen. To this day, shrimpers and fishermen entering the harbor often see a shadowy form waving a lantern back and forth on the Casablanca's widow's walk.

But, it's not just fishermen who see the old lady. Inside the inn, she is often seen or felt. Recently, a guest took a picture of herself in a mirror, and when she had the film developed, there was the ethereal figure of an old woman standing beside her.

Other guests and the owners, too, have had experiences. Items get moved or mysteriously disappear, only to reappear again in unexplainable places. Her presence is often felt in the hallways and on the stairs, but she isn't threatening. In fact, she seems to be quite friendly. I'm sure she is quite pleased with the renovation that has recently taken place.

*I*N THE 1930S NOT LONG BEFORE the beginning of the Second World War, two middle-aged sisters lived in a second-floor apartment on Hope Street. The owner and his family lived below. There was a private inside stairway to the second floor and a balcony across the length of the house facing the street, British-style, although the house had been built much later, probably in the late 1800s.

The sisters were quiet women, very fastidious and tidy. They kept a neat, clean house, although they did have a little dog, part Pekinese, part terrier, named Gerald. The dog stayed on the balcony and was not allowed in the house except when it was very cold or raining. They fed him on the balcony and walked him morning and night, so he was no trouble and didn't dirty the apartment.

They were pleasant women, but kept pretty much to themselves. Both had good jobs, and their only activities besides work seemed to be cleaning their apartment, taking care of Gerald, and reading. They had quite a sizable library and had it organized, using the Dewey Decimal System, of course.

One evening they came home, and, just as they were putting the key in the lock, heard shuffling noises from inside the house. Alarmed, they slowly opened the door. No one was there and nothing seemed amiss. Nothing was out of place, and Gerald was curled up in his little bed on the balcony.

The noise occurred again several nights later and increased in frequency, so that soon it was an almost daily occurrence. It would always stop, however, when the women opened the door. This unsettled them, but they weren't frightened, not yet.

Then, one evening they returned home first to hear the noise, and, when they opened the door, to find food crumbs on the kitchen floor. Crumbs on the floor unnerved them. Their first thought was to blame each other for failing to clean up, but they both knew that was ridiculous. They had never left cleaning chores undone. No, there had to be another explanation.

Now, both the noise and the crumbs began occurring with increasing regularity. Next, they started finding their carefully catalogued books rearranged and some even on the floor. After several weeks of these almost nightly incidents, one of the sisters became frightened and moved out. Still, the remaining sister hung on. She wasn't going to be driven from her home.

Two months passed with almost nightly occurrences of noises, food crumbs on the floor, and rearranged books. The remaining sister, now alone in the house, wasn't quite as confident as she had been. But she was stubborn, and she wouldn't be frightened away. It was probably just a friend playing pranks, anyway, she thought. Then, one night she was awakened from a sound sleep by Gerald, whose barking could only be described as hysterical. He was racing up and down the balcony in a frenzy. As the woman watched, the balcony door slowly opened, and Gerald raced in and jumped into her bed, quivering. Startled, she bolted upright in bed and watched as a white-gloved hand turned the door knob and opened the bedroom door. She leaped out of bed, ran to the door, and pulled it wide open. No one was there. She turned on the hall light but could see no one. Cautiously, she went through the entire apartment and could find no one. No windows or doors were open, or even unlocked. Gerald was still shaking in her bed.

Finally, like her sister, she'd had enough. She moved out the next day. No one knows who the ghost was or whether he remained. Both sisters and the owner are long since dead, and the house has been sold and resold several times.

*B*ERT LOOKED OUT HIS BEDROOM window on the third floor and smiled. A car had pulled up and stopped right in front of his house. Four young women got out and walked toward the front door. Gloria Smith, the realtor who managed the property, was with them. Was he getting some new boarders? He certainly hoped so. It had been so long since he'd had anyone in the house. He was lonely. He walked over to the mirror on the back of the door, adjusted his tie and the carnation in his lapel and strode happily downstairs to greet them.

He stood on the second floor landing and watched as the door opened, and the four young women bounced into the front hall with the realtor. He was overjoyed. So full of life and energy and so happy. They laughed and chatted, making jokes with one another. Bert was beside himself.

The realtor immediately began telling them how he had

built the house back in the '20s and about all the gay times the house had seen. Thank goodness she didn't mention that he had been murdered on the third floor. A nasty business, that. As the realtor showed them around the first floor, Bert followed along, listening carefully to catch everyone's name. Knowing their names was important to him. It showed he was really interested in them. Bert thought it was the only polite way to treat people.

As they walked through the sitting room, huge dining room, and into the kitchen, they all seemed to like it. They continued smiling and chatting, 'oohing' and 'ahhing.' And he'd caught some of their names. When they went into the kitchen, Victoria, the especially pretty one with long black hair, looked around, critically at first, then smiled. She liked it. Well, after all, thought Bert, it was an exceptional kitchen. He had been quite a good cook himself—when he had been alive. And, of course, he had had Chi Fong and Mrs. Hydeman to handle the parties and the big dinners. Yes, it was quite a nice kitchen. He was pleased that this Victoria liked it.

Soon, they were on the second floor. All four of them were awed by the beautiful view of the ocean and the beach from his study on the northeast corner of the house. The one named Anne seemed interested in his book collection. It was out-of-date now, but he had selected each volume with great care. Anne walked out of the library and into the adjoining bedroom. Moments later she returned with a happy, triumphant look on her face. "That's mine," she said. "I want that bedroom. It's perfect for me." Bert was pleased about that, too. He knew she wanted it because it was so close to the study. Oh, it would be so wonderful having these girls around, he thought. Perhaps, perhaps, he could establish . . . a relationship with them, nothing romantic, of course. He laughed to himself. No, not under these circumstances. But a . . . a relationship. "Get hold of yourself, Bertie. Don't count your chickens and all that." He followed after the women as they went up to the third floor.

Finally, they came to his room. It was his favorite, even though he'd been murdered there. It was a large room with plenty of space for a settee and a Victrola. And the windows reached almost to the ceiling. There was even a window seat on the west side. At night he would sit in that window and look at the lights of St. Augustine off to the southeast. He often played his Victrola. And he would waltz around the room. Oh, my, how he loved to dance.

Victoria was the first one in the room. "Oh, this is lovely," she gasped. She whirled around. "I've got to have this room." Lynne and Brenda, the other two who hadn't made any choices yet, just looked at each other and shrugged. This would be Victoria's room. Bert stood in the background and almost fainted with joy. He would have Victoria right there with him. Already she was his favorite. Then he gasped when he realized the implications. It would be very awkward living in the same room. Well, of course, he could stay out of the way, but, well, it just would be awkward.

Finally, they seemed to have made their decision. Yes, they wanted the house. The realtor shook her head happily, and the girls babbled excitedly as they moved back downstairs. It seemed to be all settled as they went out the door. Bert had followed closely behind them all the way down and now he stood in the front hall, so happy he thought his heart would burst. If he had been alive, he would have cried. After several moments, he glided back upstairs to his room, barely touching the steps as he went. He was ecstatic. He turned on his Victrola, put on a record of Viennese waltzes, and danced unrestrainedly around the room.

He didn't know when the girls would move in, but he wanted to be ready. Everything had to be perfect. The next morning he sat down at his desk and wrote a note to each young woman welcoming her to the house, adding a personal touch to each note. To Victoria, he said that he hoped she would enjoy her room as much as the original owner had. To Anne, he mentioned the study. To

Brenda, the beach, and to Lynne, the lighthouse across the bay. Then, he placed each note on a convenient table in each of the rooms the girls had chosen. He also found four vases; he planned to put fresh-cut flowers in them right before they arrived. Next, he set the dining room table for four. He wanted to prepare a wonderful dinner for them, but he knew that would be difficult and inappropriate. For now, this would be satisfactory.

Two days later, on Friday morning, the realtor returned and removed the multilock. Bert knew then that the girls would soon move in. It wouldn't take much effort, he didn't think. Over the years a lot of his furniture and other things had been removed, but the big items, like the dining room table, beds, and most of the dishes were still there. So, he was almost certain that they would each bring few of their own belongings. Saturday would be the day, he told himself. Saturday was it.

The next morning he was about early. He wanted to keep a sharp eye out for them, because he wanted to wait until the last minute to cut the flowers. Bert waited in the living room staring out the front window. Sure enough, at nine o'clock, a blue Honda pulled up. Victoria got out of the car. Bert raced out to the garden in back, going right through the walls and not even bothering to open any doors. Quickly, he cut an armful of roses, ivy, and fern— enough for four small arrangements and a larger one for the dining room. Then he charged back into the house.

Victoria had already come in, dropped a bag in the hall, and gone back out for another load. Bert quickly put flowers in the big vase on the dining room table. Then he swiftly glided upstairs and made arrangements in each of the girls rooms. He smiled and hummed softly to himself as he worked. He was very happy.

When he returned to the living room, Anne and Lynne were there. Victoria called from the dining room, "Would you two come look at this. Isn't this thoughtful?" The two walked into the dining room and saw the table arrangement.

"Did Brenda do this?"

"It had to be Brenda or Gloria."

"Well, it certainly is nice."

Bert beamed as he stood silently in the corner.

The three women went back to their unpacking and Brenda arrived a short time later. A few minutes afterward, they discovered their flowers and note cards. They were all pleased but curious.

"I think it's a wonderful thought, but I didn't do it," Brenda confided.

"Then it must have been Gloria. We'll have to call her and thank her."

They didn't have to. Just before lunch Gloria came to the door to see how the move was coming. Bert stood on the stairs as Anne answered the bell.

"Gloria," she cried, "come on in."

"Just came by to see how you were doing."

" We're slowly getting settled," Anne answered as they walked down the hall toward the kitchen. "And it was so thoughtful of you to set the table and leave the notes and flowers. Thank you so much."

Gloria stopped and look quizzically at Anne. "What are you talking about?" she asked.

"Why, didn't you leave flowers and notes in each of our rooms and set the dining room table?"

"No, dear, I didn't."

"Well, I wonder who did."

By this time the three other girls had come down and all looked at each other curiously. Bert stood in the doorway of the kitchen and could hardly contain himself. He had to stifle a large guffaw.

"It wasn't any of us," the other three added.

Anne was puzzled. "Who would have known I liked that study so much?"

Victoria looked at her wryly. "Maybe it was the owner."

"Don't be silly. He's..." She stopped in midsentence. "...dead."

The first few days passed uneventfully. The girls were busy establishing their routines and working. Bert flitted around, happy to have people in the house, to hear the sounds of someone talking. He was content just to be near them. He did have one small problem; he normally slept on the bed which Victoria now occupied. For the moment that was impossible without alerting her to his presence, so he managed on the window seat. It wasn't very comfortable, however.

One evening a week after the girls moved in, Lynne and Victoria were sitting on the sofa in the living room chatting and watching television. Bert sat nearby in the high-backed Queen Anne's chair, listening. The two women seemed to be enjoying each other's company so much and seemed so happy, Bert suddenly felt lonely. He wanted to be part of this small family. He decided to chance it.

Slowly, he eased himself into their consciousness. They couldn't yet see him, but they could feel his presence. Abruptly, they stopped talking and looked at each other.

Victoria looked at Lynne out of the corner of her eye and hesitantly asked, "Do you feel something?"

Lynne looked at Victoria with a sheepish grin. "Yes, yes. Like someone is watching us. Like there is someone in this room."

"Yes, someone else is here." Victoria looked around. "I don't feel threatened, but there is someone here. I wonder if this place is haunted."

Lynne shuddered. "I hope not. Even if it's friendly, I hope not."

Bert sensed that he was starting to alarm the girls, and he

withdrew. Pity, he thought, this may be more difficult than I planned.

The following Saturday morning, Lynne and Brenda came down to the kitchen quite early. Bert sensed them moving about and followed them. Brenda chattered away while Lynne made coffee and heated two bagels in the microwave. Now, there was a contraption that would have been useful to me, Bert said to himself. When the coffee was finished, the girls poured themselves steaming cups and went out to sit on the back porch and watch the sun come up over their beautiful beach. Bert decided to try again.

Lynne took a sip of coffee and put her cup down. "Do you smell carnations, Brenda?"

Brenda sniffed. "Yes, I do. That's really strange." She stood and looked out in the garden to see if carnations were planted anywhere. "That is really strange."

"You know, the other night Vickie and I were watching TV, and we both had the sensation that someone was in the room with us."

Bert sat on a table just behind them and listened. He earnestly hoped they would give some indication of wanting to make contact.

"I wonder if this place is haunted."

"I asked the same thing. Scary, isn't it?"

"Scary," Brenda asserted. "Scary isn't the word for it. If this place is haunted, even if it's the ghost of Mother Theresa, I'm gone."

"Oh, Brenda, don't be an idiot. Mother Theresa isn't even dead yet."

"I don't care who it is. I just couldn't handle a ghost."

Bert sighed. He had struck out again. This was so sad, he thought. Why were people so close-minded? He wasn't some fiendish demon who wanted to snatch their souls. He was just a lonely spirit searching for companionship. People, living ones, were sometimes so thoughtless.

Well, he would just have to try again.

Bert felt uncomfortable. He enjoyed having these four young women in the house. He enjoyed hearing their laughter and their talk. He loved the old, familiar smells that came from an active kitchen. He relished the hustle and bustle and confusion of mealtimes with all four girls there. Sometimes, they invited friends, and Bert was reminded of the lively dinner parties he once had hosted. It was very nostalgic, and he was very happy that they were all there, but he wanted more. He wanted real contact.

He drifted from one room to another, longing for their companionship and wondering what to do. He was walking a fine line. He didn't want to frighten them away, but he had to have more. He decided that he had to risk trying again.

He hadn't approached Anne yet, and she seemed to be quite stable. He would try her. It was Friday night. Anne was going out and was sitting at her dressing table putting on makeup. He walked up behind her and started to materialize, being very careful to smile and appear non-threatening. She looked up in her mirror and saw him. Her face froze in a horrified look, and she spun around. He melted from sight. He could hear her gasp, her breath almost a panting. Soon, she calmed herself and turned back around.

After a few minutes, Bert again slowly materialized. This time, when Anne saw him, she screamed and ran out of the room.

"Oh, dear," he said aloud as he followed her out of the room.

Anne ran, gasping, down the stairs to the living room where the other girls were watching TV. They had heard her scream and were all standing with worried looks.

"I . . . I . . . saw a ghost. I actually saw a ghost," she stammered, trying to catch her breath. "There was a ghost in my room. I saw it in my mirror."

Victoria took her by the arm. "Here, Anne, sit down a minute and try to calm yourself. Now try to relax. Brenda, get her a cup of coffee, will you? No, make it a glass of wine."

"I don't want any wine," Anne shouted angrily. "I saw a ghost, I tell you."

"What did he look like, Anne?"

Anne sat silent for a moment, not moving, not saying anything. Then she took two deep breaths. "I was sitting at my dressing table, putting on lipstick. When I looked up, I saw him. Standing right behind me. I saw him in the mirror. I spun around quickly, and he was gone. But when I turned back to the mirror, there he was again. That's when I screamed and ran down here."

"Yes, but what did he look like? Can you describe him?"

Well, he . . . he was quite handsome, really. And he was smiling. I was just so surprised. He was clean shaven and had on a suit and tie. In fact, the collar was one of those stiff things my grandfather used to wear. Oh, he was wearing a hat. And . . . and he had a carnation in his lapel."

Lynne and Brenda looked wide-eyed at each other. "We were sitting on the back porch a couple of Saturdays back and smelled carnations. It was really spooky."

Victoria jumped in. "Now, let's not all get hysterical over this. There must be some logical explanation. Let's be sensible."

Bert stood in the doorway and nodded agreement. Yes, let's be sensible, he thought. I'm not going to hurt anyone. I don't even want to frighten anyone. He walked over to his Queen Anne's chair and sat down.

Anne returned later in the evening and, in fact, slept in her own room, even though Bert could see that she was a bit jumpy. Actually, everyone was a bit jumpy for several days. Gradually, however, the girls settled down, and everything seemed to be back to normal. Perhaps, he should try again, he thought.

One Saturday afternoon Victoria was lying down resting. Bert walked over to the bed and gently shook her. She hardly stirred, so he shook her again. This time she sat upright and looked angrily around the room. Oh, dear, Bert thought, now I've upset her. Victoria raced downstairs and out onto the back porch, demanding to know who had interrupted her sleep.

"Vickie, we've all been sitting right here for the last half hour or so," Lynne answered.

Brenda was alarmed. "What happened, Vickie?"

Victoria wilted into a chair. "Someone shook me awake. I was sound asleep, and someone woke me up."

"This is getting too spooky for me," Brenda said, and she jumped out of her chair and headed for the door.

"Now, wait a minute, Brenda, don't wig out on us. Maybe, I imagined all this. Maybe I just dreamed it. I mean, I didn't see anything."

"Geez. This is too weird."

"I know, but let's let it be for now, okay?"

Bert stood there, dejected. He had only wanted to make contact, to have someone to be with. But he had succeeded only in upsetting the girls. Oh, dear, dear, he thought. I've made a mess of things. And he wondered off back up to the third floor.

That night, after everyone had gone to bed, Bert sat at the window seat and looked out at the lights of St. Augustine. He couldn't sleep. He felt lonelier now than he had before the girls had come. He botched this whole thing up, terribly, terribly. Now, what could he do? He sat there most of the night, worrying, feeling sorry for himself. By early morning he was exhausted. Without thinking, he walked over to the bed and lay down. Victoria, who was on the other side of the bed, must have felt the pressure. She seemed to wake up. Could she hear him breathing? She reached out to feel his side of the bed, and Bert rolled off onto the floor. She must have felt that, too, because she jumped out of bed and flicked on the lights. She grabbed a bathrobe and put it on. Then she headed toward the door.

Bert was panic-stricken. He stood up and materialized. "Please don't go," he begged. "Please stay."

Victoria looked in horror at him, put her hand to her mouth, screamed, and ran out the door. Moments later he heard all four girls talking excitedly. Then, he heard the front door close and their four cars drive away. The next day they returned with seven or eight others, and by noon they were gone, moved out. Bert was alone again.

Every once in a while, at dusk, Bert will see a blue Honda pass by, and he'll flip lights on, hoping that it's Victoria, but he doesn't know. Bert has been alone since then, and the house looks as sad as the ghost who lives on the third floor.

*T*HE AUGUSTIN INN ON CUNA Street, just down from the White Lion Cafe and Pub, is one of the newest bed-and-breakfast inns in St. Augustine. It was recently renovated and is an excellent lodging. Although it is new, it has quite a remarkable history.

Many years ago an elderly lady owned the house. She was a colorful character. A spinster who never married, she had several gentleman friends during her lifetime. She was a free-spirited and very independent woman who lived her life the way she wanted to live it, convention and propriety be damned. When she died of natural causes, or so the story goes, she left her house and everything in it, all her worldly possessions, to her younger brother who lived not far away.

The brother, although he and his wife and teenage daughter were saddened by her death, was very pleased to have inherited the house. It was a lovely home, and he thought seriously of moving his family into it. Besides, it was within a few minutes' walking distance from his work.

A week after the funeral, his daughter volunteered to begin the task of going through her aunt's things, sorting them out, and making an inventory, so that they could decide what to keep and what to sell. It was early on a summer morning when she walked over to her deceased aunt's house and went to work. Knowing that her father was considering moving into the house, she walked around the rooms, upstairs and down, with an eye toward a room of her own. Of course, she assumed that her parents would lay claim to the large master bedroom, but she particularly liked a smaller room in the corner, down the hall. With windows on two sides, it was well-lit and airy, and it overlooked the street and all its activity. It would be an exciting room for a teenage girl.

She tarried a few moments in the room, fantasizing about all the interesting things she might do in there if it ever got to be her room, and then she went back downstairs to begin sorting. In the small back room that had been her aunt's study, she found stacks and stacks of old papers and magazines; her aunt wasn't really a very neat person. First, in one of the piles she found an old Ouija board. This is really weird, she thought. She wasn't exactly certain what a Ouija board was or how to use it, but she knew it was something strange, so she set it aside. She continued sifting through each pile of papers and magazines, throwing most away and placing the rest in neat stacks. Then she came to a stack that contained several weird magazines. This was really too strange, and she got up and went back home, taking the Ouija board and mysterious magazines with her.

Her mother was alarmed when she saw the board and magazines, but her father, when he came home, just shook his head. As he told his wife and daughter, his sister was a bit of a kook, and he wasn't at all surprised to see such things. The three laughed about it, but the husband took the precaution of removing the items from the house and throwing them in a public trash disposal down the street.

The next day the girl went back to continue her work. This time, however, she felt a little odd and even nervous. She was downright jumpy, in fact. Shortly after she arrived and went back into her aunt's study, she heard a thumping noise, then another and another. The noise came from the second floor. It couldn't have been a squirrel on the roof, or even on the second floor, for that matter. It was much too loud. If it had been a squirrel, she wouldn't have even heard it. When the noise continued, she became frightened and ran home.

Breathless, she recounted what had happened to her mother who thought perhaps she was hearing things. Maybe the conversation of the previous evening about her aunt's Ouija board had activated her young imagination. When her father came home later, he smiled and reassured her that she probably hadn't heard anything or, if she had, the noise could easily be explained. He also suggested that his wife accompany her when she went back.

So the next day, mother and daughter went over to the empty house to finish the job. As soon as they unlocked the front door and walked into the house, the thumping noise started again, this time louder and quicker. Startled and terrified, they ran out of the house. Neither would go upstairs to find out what or who was making the pounding noise.

The father listened to their tale that evening and decided he must get involved and settle whatever the problem was. The next day was Saturday, so, after breakfast, he took his Smith & Wesson .357 and went to the house by himself, a brave thing to do. Wearily, he searched every room, upstairs and down. He found nothing, absolutely nothing.

Puzzled he thought about what might be causing the thumping noises. He just couldn't figure it out. Then he remembered a friend of the family, a psychic. Surely, she could put an end to this. He called her, and that afternoon she came over. While the husband, his wife, and his daughter stood in the street and waited, the psychic went into the house. She was there more than an hour, walking slowly through each of the rooms. Finally, she came outside.

"Yes, you have a presence. A spirit has recently taken up residence here," she said.

"Well, can you tell us something about it? What is it, or who is it?" the man asked.

The psychic explained, "It's a man, an older gentleman. He has white hair and a close-cropped, white beard; rather a tall man."

Husband and wife looked at each other. "Oh, my gosh," they said in unison. "That's Chiles," the wife said with a shudder. Chiles was her sister-in-law's last boyfriend. He had died two years before. Neither of them liked him. They thought he was pompous, lazy, and good for nothing. The feeling was mutual; he hadn't liked them either. With Chiles around, they would have to rethink their plan of moving into the house.

It was getting late, so the husband went back in, made sure all the lights were off, and they left. The psychic returned home, and the family went to dinner at the Columbia on Hypolita. When they left the restaurant, it was dark, and they walked down Cuna Street on their way home. As they passed the house, they noticed one of the upstairs lights on. Funny, the husband was sure he'd turned them all off. Nevertheless, the light was on. He would just have to go up and turn it off. He unlocked the door and entered the house; the foyer light came on, even before he could reach for the switch. He walked toward the stairs, and the stair lights came on, again before he even reached out for the switch. Then all the lights downstairs illuminated, and, as he walked upstairs, all of the second floor lights came on. That was enough for him. He turned around on the stairs and left.

Their decision was made. They would sell the house and everything in it. They never went near the place again, even to show the place to prospective buyers. The daughter was unhappy about not getting that wonderful room for her own, but she decided that, perhaps, it would have been a little too exciting.

Although the presence which occupied the house was not particularly threatening, subsequent owners did have a few experiences with him and finally had the house exorcised. Chiles has apparently found a new home, because no one has had any unusual encounters since.

I don't know the difference between a ghost and an angel; some say that a ghost is the spirit of a human and an angel a heavenly body. I'm not so sure. I have heard many stories of ghosts who acted a lot like angels. This story is about one of them.

MARGARET MATTHEWS WOKE UP when her bedroom door opened. Rising up on her elbows she saw a small figure in a nightgown glide toward her bed. It was Katie. Katie was her granddaughter, who was visiting for a week while her parents, Margaret's daughter, Bev, and her husband, Jim, had a week to themselves up in the North Carolina mountains.

Margaret lived for her two daughters and their children, and she loved to have company, especially her grandchildren. Both of Susan's girls were grown and living out of state, but Bev still had little Katie, and Margaret loved to have her around. Since her husband Harold had died, this old house on Charlotte Street was lonely—lonely and sad. Katie was a dear. She was such a bright and cheerful child. And as the youngest of all the grandchildren, she was Margaret's favorite, not that she didn't love them all, but Katie was the last, and she was special.

Katie padded next to her grandmother's bed. "Gramma, I don't feel so well. Can I sleep with you?"

"Of course, you can, darling," Margaret cooed as she lifted up the covers and helped the child into bed. "Do you feel sick, sweetheart?" Margaret asked, and she felt Katie's forehead. "Oh, my goodness. You have a little fever. Let me take your temperature." Margaret got out of bed and went to the bathroom for a thermometer while Katie talked in her forlorn little voice.

"I have a headache, Gramma, and I ache. I won't throw up, though."

Margaret returned, switched on the light, and placed the thermometer into the little girl's mouth. She waited a couple of minutes, then took it out and looked at it. It registered one hundred and one. "Oh, for mercy's sake, you do have a fever. Well, I'll just get you an aspirin and some water, and you'll feel fine in the morning."

She got the water and the aspirin, gave it to Katie, and tucked her in. Katie snuggled down and smiled up at her grandmother. "Thank you, Gramma. I love you."

Margaret smiled back and turned out the light. "I love you, too, Katie."

Sometime later Margaret woke again. She was a little worried about Katie who now slept soundly beside her. As she turned toward the child to feel her forehead she saw something at the end of the bed. There was the shadowy figure of a man dressed all in white sitting cross-legged on the floor. Even though it was pitch black in the room, she could see him clearly as though he were covered by a soft, white light. He was just sitting there, facing the bed, not looking at anything.

Amazingly, his presence did not disturb her. Instead, she felt perfectly comfortable with him in the room. She knew somehow that the presence was a spirit and not a living human being, and yet, she wasn't frightened by it. She had never believed in ghosts. She'd certainly never had any experiences with them, but she knew absolutely that this was a spiritual being. She supposed that she should have been frightened, but she wasn't. Then a strange thought came to her. Could this be Katie's guardian angel? She lay back down, peaceful, and went to sleep.

In the morning, not long before daylight, she woke, roused herself, and got out of bed. She felt rested and thought of the spirit, or angel, or whatever it was. "Did that really happen?" she thought to herself. But she knew the answer; she knew it had. She couldn't see anything in the room, but she felt a warmth, a presence that comforted her.

She looked down at Katie, who slept soundly. Poor child must be exhausted, Margaret thought. She went quietly downstairs to make coffee.

As she sat in her kitchen drinking her first cup of coffee and enjoying the tranquillity of the early morning, she heard Katie cry out. Rushing upstairs, she went into the bedroom to comfort the child.

"Here, sweetheart, let's take that temperature again," she said as she turned on the light and put the thermometer in the girl's mouth. Her temperature had risen to one hundred and four. Margaret was alarmed. Too high, she thought, we've got to get her temperature down. "Will you be all right, Katie? I'm going down to get you some juice. I'll be back in a minute."

"I'll be okay, Gramma," Katie whimpered.

Margaret turned to go out the door and there, only faintly visible, was the angel, now standing at the foot of the bed looking at Katie. Margaret could barely see him. He was like a hologram at

Disney, but there he was. Intuitively, she knew that he was watching over the little girl. She looked at the spirit, then at her granddaughter. Apparently, Katie had no idea he was there.

Margaret was worried about Katie's temperature. At first, she thought about calling Bev but decided against it. Calling would only upset her daughter, and there was nothing she could do about it. No, best to call her doctor, John Craig, and she picked up the phone.

Such a wonderful man, she thought. He hadn't even had his breakfast yet, but he came right over. Fortunately, he lived only two blocks away on Marine Street.

Margaret answered Dr. Craig's knock at the door. "Thank you so much for coming over, John," she said.

"No problem, Margaret. Where's Katie?"

"Upstairs. She's sleeping for the moment. It's probably nothing to worry about, but she does have a temperature of one hundred and four."

"No. No. You're right, Margaret. Best not to take any chances. Let's go have a look at her."

Softly, they opened the door and walked into the room. Margaret switched on the light next to Katie's side of the bed. She could see the spirit on the opposite side, even fainter than he was before. She looked at Dr. Craig. Could he see the angel? she wondered. The doctor showed no reaction, and the spirit just stood there.

Katie was awake and said hello to Dr. Craig. Apparently, she didn't seem to be aware of the presence either. The doctor took her temperature again, checked her with a stethoscope, and looked her over.

"I don't think there's anything to worry about," he said, giving Katie a gentle pat on the head. "Here, I'll give you some of these," and he rummaged through his bag. "They're a little stronger than aspirin. Make sure she gets plenty of rest, and make her drink a lot—water, juice, whatever she likes. She should be fine in a day or two."

Margaret walked the doctor downstairs and to the door.

"Thanks so much, John."

"My pleasure, Margaret. Don't worry. She'll be fine. Call me if anything changes." And he walked out the door and down the steps. Margaret closed the door softly behind him and hurried back up to Katie.

Margaret opened the blinds. She helped Katie sit up in bed and fluffed the pillows behind her. The angel moved to the foot of the bed and stood still. Margaret looked at the spirit, then at Katie. She was astounded that she herself was not frightened or that Katie did not acknowledge the presence. This is crazy, she thought.

"I'll go down and get you some breakfast, dear. What would you like?"

"I'm not real hungry, Gramma, but I would like some juice."

"How about some orange juice, a cup of hot tea with honey in it, and some toast with marmalade?"

"Okay, Gramma. I'd like that."

Margaret returned a short time later with Katie's breakfast. She had also gone to the spare room where Katie had been sleeping and retrieved several of the child's books and dolls. "Here, darling. I also brought you this little bell. I've got some things to do downstairs. If you need me, just ring the bell."

"Thank you, Gramma," she said as she began nibbling at her breakfast.

Margaret left the room to tend to her chores. The angel remained at the foot of the little girl's bed.

Margaret got involved writing letters and doing some cleaning. She was cleaning in the kitchen when she happened to look up at the clock. "Oh, for mercy's sake," she said aloud. It was ten o'clock already, and Katie hadn't rung once. She poured another glass of juice and went upstairs to check on her granddaughter. Katie was sitting up talking to one of her dolls. The angel was still at the foot of the bed.

"How are you doing, dear? Feeling any better?"

Katie looked up. "Hi, Gramma. We're playing."

"Yes, I can see that," Margaret smiled. "Here. I've brought you some more juice. Need anything else?"

"No. Thanks, Gramma."

Margaret gave her granddaughter a little hug and walked out of the room.

Several times during the day, she went up to check on Katie, taking her lunch and juice. Each time she went into the room, the spirit was there. Most often he just stood at the end of the bed, but once he was sitting cross-legged on the floor by Katie and another time he was actually sitting on the bed. Oddly, Margaret was quite comfortable with him there, and Katie seemed to be oblivious to his presence.

Katie stayed in bed two more days, slowly recovering. The angel was constantly nearby. Then, the third morning when Margaret woke up and went to check on Katie. The spirit was gone. Katie was still sleeping soundly. At first, Margaret was alarmed because the angel wasn't there. Then she thought that might be a good sign. Sure enough, when Katie awoke later, she was fine and apparently had had no idea that an angel had kept a vigil over her.

At the end of the week her parents returned to pick her up, and as Margaret was relating the events of the past few days without mentioning the spirit, the little girl nonchalantly looked at her mother and said, "Mommy, did you know I have a guardian angel?" Margaret was astounded; Katie had seen the spirit.

Bev smiled down at Katie. "Of course, you do, darling. We all do." Margaret laughed to herself and thought, "Beverly, you have no idea."

*H*AROLD'S FAMILY USED TO OWN A home on Spring Street. Not long after his grandfather's family moved into the house around the time of the First World War, they began hearing strange, unaccountable noises and feeling the presence of something no one could explain. Most of the activity centered around one room, a bedroom where the girls slept.

According to the young daughters, something would lift them out of their beds and throw them to the floor. Harold's grandfather thought they were silly, and after two or three occurrences when the girls came crying to his room in the middle of the night, he decided to sleep in the room himself. He was a very heavy sleeper, and he didn't wake up all night. But in the morning, he found himself on the floor underneath the bed.

When Harold's mother was about three years old, his grandmother miscarried twins and became deathly ill with toxemia. Late one winter evening after it was already dark and before her husband returned home, she took a turn for the worse. She was a very religious woman, and she began praying. As she prayed she heard singing far off in the distance. The music came from a window. Dragging herself to the window, she looked out and saw a figure floating down and singing an eerie little tune. The words to the song were, "Good for you, ha, ha, ha, good for you." Even though it was in a minor chord, it was very comforting to her. Soon, her husband arrived and took her to the hospital, where she recovered. Harold's mother grew up with this little song, for his grandmother sang it often after that, this little song given to her by what she referred to as "her angel."

Almost twenty years later, around Christmas, Harold's grandfather had a serious stroke and was taken to the hospital. The Florida East Coast Hospital used to be next to the present police station, and he was taken there. It was a very bad stroke, and he was in critical condition. Harold's grandmother rode in the ambulance, and his mother followed in a separate car. They stayed with him for a while but finally were asked to leave by the hospital staff. He was sleeping, and there was nothing more they could do.

When they left it was dark, foggy, and cold outside. As the two women walked down the steps of the hospital they heard a soft voice singing. It was the same simple little song Harold's grandmother had heard those many years before. They looked at each other and raced back inside. They got to the room just as Harold's grandfather drew his last breath. To this day, both Harold's mother and his grandmother are convinced that "her angel" had come down to take their father and husband away.

On nearby Arenta Street there is another house where Harold has encountered ghostly activity. A young man named David had a room in the house. One evening David, Harold, and a couple of others stopped by on their way to a party. They had been at the beach, and David wanted to change before going on. David got out of the car, while Harold and the others waited.

Harold and his friends sat in the car talking. A few moments later they saw David's light come on. After several minutes the lights in David's room started flashing on and off, and his friends thought he was trying to be funny. Shortly after, David came rushing out, breathless and a little distraught.

He related that he'd taken a quick shower and changed his clothes. As he was walking across the room, the lights went out, and something grabbed him. It wouldn't let go. He struggled for several seconds and pushed toward the door. Finally he broke loose and ran out into the hall. As he was going down the hall, the lights there went out, and something touched his back. That's when he raced out. David later learned that a man had been shot and killed in the hallway many years before.

Harold and another friend, Gary, also had an experience in the house. The two and several others had spent the evening with David in the house, just "hanging out," as young people will do. The hour grew late, so, instead of going home, they decided to stay. There were enough couches and empty beds. Harold and Gary found themselves on couches in the living room.

The next morning, groggy with sleep, Harold and Gary looked at each other. "Did you notice anything last night?" Harold asked.

"Yes, I did. I woke up in the middle of the night, and it sounded like there was a party going on in here. I heard people talking and laughing, glasses tinkling. It sounded like the room was full of people. But when I looked around, of course, it was dark, and you and I were the only ones here."

"Hmmm, I woke up, too. I heard sounds like furniture being moved around or slid across the floor. It was really spooky."

Almost without exception the ghosts and spirits dwelling in St. Augustine are as benign as Casper. Like the living inhabitants, they seem to be tempered by the strife and struggles of the city's long history. However, there are exceptions, and this story about a passage to hell, which was related to me by a nervous young woman, is one of them.

I RECEIVED A CALL FROM A YOUNG woman who had heard that I was writing about the ghosts of St. Augustine. She said she had something interesting to tell me. We met for coffee on Aviles Street. After we introduced ourselves, we sat down and ordered coffee and sandwiches.

We talked for a few minutes about trivial things. She asked what I thought of St. Augustine and told me that she was a native. Then I asked what she had to tell me. At first, she was silent. I waited. Finally, she took a deep breath and began talking very softly, as if she were afraid someone might hear. "My friend, Carol, in the studio just down the street, told me you were writing a book about the ghosts here."

"Why, yes, I know Carol. Nice lady. She gave me the names of several people." I paused. "Although, she never mentioned yours."

"Well, I've been reluctant to say anything about this. It was so terrifying. I still have nightmares, and it's been almost seven years. Maybe telling you will help."

She looked around again, and in an even quieter voice she continued, "Back in the late eighties my husband and I—we were newlyweds at the time—rented a small house over on the Island. The house was only about ten years old. It was a nice little place, two bedrooms, central air. The garage had been converted into a laundry room and workshop, but a carport had been added shortly before we moved in."

She fidgeted with her coffee cup and looked down into it, pausing. "The laundry room," she sighed. "That was the problem. Well, anyway, it seemed like a very nice place, and we could afford the rent, so we took it. And everything was fine for the first few days. My husband had taken a vacation, and we were busy moving in and arranging things.

"Then, the following Monday, the Monday after we moved in, my husband went back to work, and I was alone in the house for the first time. I had fixed him breakfast, and after he left, I started cleaning house. First, I cleaned up after breakfast. Then, I went into the laundry room to start a load of wash, and I got the strangest feeling. My spine began tingling, and I felt this presence. It was physical, like some giant person was hugging me, a pressure all around me, like, like being underwater twenty or thirty feet. It wasn't uncomfortable. It was just very strange. And I felt cold, too. Really weird.

"Well, I got the washing started and went back into the other part of the house. I was back in the laundry room three or four times that day, putting things in and taking them out of the washer and dryer, and each time I was in there, I got this weird sensation." She stopped talking for a moment and fumbled with her coffee cup, as though she were remembering.

"I told Jim—that's my husband—about it that evening, and he just thought I was a little anxious about being alone after spending so much time with him during the wedding and honeymoon and all. But he understood, and we talked about it. Then he suggested that we go into the laundry room together. I didn't want to, but he insisted, so we went in. I felt nothing. Neither did Jim. In fact, he was in the room for perhaps an hour, puttering around, and he didn't experience anything. At least, he didn't admit it. So, I just let it pass.

"But the next day, Tuesday, I found myself avoiding going into the laundry room. Silly, I guess, but I didn't want to go in there. Then, on Wednesday I had to go in, and the same darned thing happened. Only this time, it was worse." She shuddered.   "This time it wasn't just a gentle hug, it was a constricting, icy cold grip. I could hardly move, and I was almost shivering from the cold. I panicked and broke free from it. Ran out of the room. Out of the house onto the front porch and just sat, trying to catch my breath and almost in tears." She stopped again to collect herself.

"That's when the lady next door came over. She introduced herself, and we chatted. She was nice, an older woman. She and her husband were both retired. Then, I guess she saw I was upset and asked if anything was the matter. So, I told her what had just happened to me. Well, she just looked at me, then at the house with this real serious look."

"'You know, something like that happened to the last people who lived here. The woman was in the laundry room and said she was overcome by an awful fear—like Amityville. She just ran out of the house, terrified. I found her sitting out by that tree, crying her eyes out. Never would go back. They moved the next day. Her husband had to do all the packing. She wouldn't go near the place. I've never been in there myself. Some strange goings on, if you ask me. Well, anyway, come on over and have some coffee. It'll calm your nerves.'"

The young woman stopped and looked at me, her eyes questioning. "Is this weird or what?" she asked.

I chuckled. "Yes, it's weird, but it's certainly believable."

She continued. "I spent an hour or more with my neighbor and finally went home. I didn't go into the laundry again. I was afraid. When Jim came home that evening, I tried to act as nonchalant as possible. I didn't tell him what had happened, and he didn't ask.

"Well, everything was okay for about three weeks. Nothing much happened. Of course, I used the laundry room, and every time I went in, I felt a presence, but it was gentle, not frightening like the first time. Then, right after Jim had left one Thursday morning, I went in to do laundry." Her voice wavered and trailed off.

I reached out and patted her hand. "It's okay," I said. "Nothing can bother you now."

We sat silent for several minutes. The waitress came by and refilled our coffee cups. The young woman stared out the window at the new building across the street.

Finally, she looked back at me and went on. "I went back in to do the laundry, and I was seized by an even more powerful force. It totally enveloped me, crushing, pulling me. I struggled. I couldn't breathe. I tried to scream, but nothing came out. The force was trying to drag me across the room. I looked over and could see this image. It was like heat waves shimmering off the pavement on a hot day, and it was sort of oval, like a doorway but oval. It reminded me

120

of the mouth of a cave, perhaps, or something like that. But it wasn't hot; the whole room was cold, icy cold, like the inside of a walk-in refrigerator. I was numb from the cold, and I couldn't breathe, and I was getting weak. This thing was dragging me toward the shimmering archway. . . . Finally, I broke free. . . . I ran from the room and out the front door . . . and stood gasping for breath on the porch.

"I could hardly stand . . . my knees shook . . . my whole body was shaking. Eventually, I was able to get to the car. I wouldn't go back into that house for the car keys, but there was a spare set of keys in one of those little magnetic boxes, stuck under the wheel well. I got them and drove into town." She stopped talking then and composed herself.

"I stayed away for several hours. Finally, in the middle of the afternoon, I came back and cautiously went inside. Everything seemed to be okay, but I was exhausted, absolutely drained. I went into the bedroom—it was at the far end of the house—I went in, locked the door, lay down, and closed my eyes. I was asleep in minutes.

"An hour or so later, I guess it was about four o'clock, I woke up with a start. Someone was sitting on the bed. I couldn't see them, but the sheets were stretched, and I could see the indentation where someone was sitting, but there was no one there. This time I wasn't panicked; I was really mad, I'd had enough. I got up, collected my purse and a few things and went outside to wait for Jim.

"When he came home about an hour later, I told him what had happened. He immediately called a friend of his who knew a psychic, and she arrived about six. I think her name was Mona, Mona Freeman, something like that.

"Reluctantly, I went back into the house with them. I was scared to death. We walked all around the place, Mona stopping, looking at this and that, closing her eyes. Then we finally went to the laundry room. I refused to go in, the doorway was as close as I'd get. But Mona and Jim and his friend just charged right in.

—"Mona stopped abruptly in the middle of the room and was quiet, just standing there. Sometimes she'd close her eyes, sometimes she'd look around, but she stood completely still for the longest time, silent. Finally, she spoke, 'There are spirits in here, a family. There's a man and woman and young boy about eight. I think they were killed in an automobile accident about eight years ago. One of them was probably sitting on your bed, maybe trying to comfort you.' She paused, then continued, 'But that's not your problem. There is also some kind of passage, a pathway, a doorway into the spirit world, but it feels very bad. Let's go outside,' she said calmly.

"When we were back out on the porch again, she stood silent for a long time with her eyes closed, like she was trying to get in touch with something. Then she explained, 'As I was telling you about the passage, I could feel an awful demonic presence trying to get through. I don't know how long that passage will be there nor how big it will get, but it's definitely there, a sort of gateway to hell.' A gateway to hell . . . " the young woman repeated.

"We stayed in a motel that night, and, like those former residents, Jim moved us out the next day. . . . Well, that's my story. Weird, isn't it?"

"Not at all," I said. "I bet I've talked to fifty people here in town with stories just as strange. After doing the research for this book, I'd believe almost anything." Then an idea came to mind. "Would you mind going over there with me, to show me the house?"

She just shuddered, rolled her eyes, and looked at me, "You've got to be kidding. I wouldn't go near that place. Why, I won't even cross over that bridge!"

N

O ONE IS EXACTLY SURE WHERE they came from, some place up north, I suppose. No one knows. In fact, nobody is sure that their last name was Spencer or that their first names were Todd, Sarah, and Sally. The three are somewhat of a mystery, and I guess that's as it should be, because their departing was as mysterious as their arrival.

The brother and sisters appeared in St. Augustine one day and immediately set up housekeeping in a home they purchased in Vilano Beach, not far from the ocean. It was a large home, five or six bedrooms, and well-appointed. It doesn't exist anymore; it was torn down a few years ago, but old-timers remember it as one of the most splendid homes in the area.

The Spencers—we'll call them that—loved to entertain. At least once a week, and often much more, they threw lavish dinner parties which lasted late into the night. Their guests included some of the most influential people in town, although no one quite remembers how they came to be in the upper circles of local society. Still, all three were well-liked and popular, even if they had no close friends.

That brings up another mystery about Todd and his sisters. None of them seemed to do any work. No one knew where they got their money, and they certainly had lots of it to be able to entertain in such a grand style. No one cared, perhaps, not while they were sitting at the Spencer's groaning table, stuffing themselves with sumptuous treats, anyway.

They weren't young people by any means, but they weren't that old either—in their late forties or early fifties as one long-time resident seemed to remember. Todd was the oldest, or was it Sally? Well, no matter. Their ages were another mystery.

Within a year of their arrival, Todd disappeared. Sarah and Sally had a dinner party one evening, and when someone remarked about Todd's absence, the two sisters simply said that he had gone on a trip. "He'll be back," they both smiled nonchalantly, and that was it. Only trouble was, he never returned.

However, the ladies never missed a step. The parties, the music, the lights, and the late nights continued. Neighbors got used to it, and they never complained, although they often talked among themselves. Perhaps they were envious and a little jealous if they didn't get invited.

Several months later, three weeks after Christmas, Sally invited fifty people from the upper crust of St. Augustine society to a luxurious dinner party which included a nine-course banquet and dancing to a twenty-piece orchestra. It was an extravagant affair, bigger than any New Year's Eve party or any of the other balls that occurred throughout the year. There were cars and limousines with drivers parked around for blocks. Vilano Beach had never seen anything like it.

Strangely, when the guests began to arrive, only Sally was there to greet them. Odd, everyone thought. Where was Sarah? And, for that matter, why hadn't Todd returned? Sally smiled. Sarah had gone to New York to be with a sick aunt. She would return in three or four weeks. Well, the guests soon forgot about Sarah, as they had mostly forgotten about Todd, when they sat down to dinner. Sally had imported an internationally renowned chef and had hired a local caterer to provide a working staff for him. It was a smashing success.

Well, the parties continued, week after week, month after month. Sarah hadn't returned, nor had Todd, but when Sally was asked, she just smiled and explained away her brother's and sister's absence as though they had just gone to Jacksonville for the weekend.

No one is exactly sure when it happened, because the lights and the music and noise continued for a long time. But one day, a neighbor realized she hadn't seen Sally for days, or was it weeks? Very strange. She asked around. No one else in the neighborhood had seen her either. Then someone realized that, although the partying had continued, there hadn't been any unusual amount of traffic, people or automobiles. In fact, quite the opposite was true. When they thought about it, it seemed there had been fewer cars than normal.

A week later, the morning after a particularly raucous party, the next-door neighbor finally went over and knocked on Sally's door. No one answered. She knocked again and called out. Still, no one answered. She knocked and called out several more times with no response. Eventually she called the police. When a squad car arrived, she explained the circumstances, and although the officers were reluctant to break into the place with so little evidence, they received permission from their headquarters and broke through the front door.

Carefully checking each room, they found nothing downstairs. Nothing seemed amiss. Everything was in place, and there was no evidence of foul play. Then they went upstairs and continued to search room by room. The first two rooms, a study and what was probably a sitting room, were in order, nothing in disarray. When they reached the third room, what they thought to be a bedroom, the door was closed. Slowly, one of the officers turned the knob and pushed it opened.

They were almost overcome by the stench of rotting human flesh. There on the bed lay the body of what later was determined to be Sally Spencer, dead for several days. After they composed themselves and got over their initial shock they checked the room and the body over. There was no sign of violence and no wounds on the body.

The officers decided that they should check the rest of the house and started down the hall. The next room, like the last appeared to be a bedroom. Its door was also closed. With a sense of foreboding, they entered. Sarah Spencer, in a nightgown and very decomposed, lay tucked in her bed. Like her sister, she seemed to have died a nonviolent death.

The rest of the rooms along the hall were in order, but when the two officers got to the last room, a large corner room, they found Todd. He, too, was in his bed in silk pajamas. He was little more than a skeleton. By this time the coroner had arrived with ambulances and quickly took the corpses out of the house for autopsies. Subsequent forensic examination revealed that all three had died of natural causes.

The authorities returned to the house, of course, to try to find out exactly who the Spencers were and where they were from. Why had the surviving siblings left the bodies in their beds? And what about Sally? How could all three of them have died of natural causes? And how could all three of them have died in their beds? No one was ever able to find out anything. There was nothing in the house that revealed any next of kin or even any place to look. There was nothing to give any indication of the circumstances of their deaths. Not one question was ever answered. The house and its contents were eventually sold at an auction and the money given to charity.

Most mysteriously, people in Vilano Beach continued to see lights and hear the gay sounds of people laughing and dancing for years afterward. In fact, some say that they often hear noises and see lights even today, even though the house was torn down in the '80s. Perhaps they can. I don't really know. At least, it makes a good story.

ONE SUNDAY MORNING A FEW years ago the minister of the Wildwood Baptist Church stood in front of his congregation during a service and led in the singing of that beautiful old hymn, "Zion's Hill." His great voice boomed out and inspired everyone present, who joined in with equal passion. While the congregation was thus engaged in the singing, Willie Watkins and her sister happened to look behind the minister and watched as a man wearing a black suit and top hat walked in and discreetly sat in the minister's chair. Willie thought it a little strange, first that someone would come right in and sit in the minister's chair, second, that he would wear a top hat in church, and third, that no one else seemed to notice. When the hymn ended, the man suddenly wasn't there. Willie thought that was very strange.

She was afraid to ask so she didn't say anything, but after several days her curiosity overcame her fear, and she asked the minister who the man was. He smiled, "That was Mr. Anthony. He died several years ago, as you remember, and 'Zion's Hill' was his favorite song. He comes around whenever we sing it."

There have been other unexplainable occurrences at the Wildwood Baptist Church. Once a man was walking by the church and the cemetery next to it at dusk and saw the statue of an angel standing next to a fresh grave. It wasn't at the head or the foot of the grave; it was right in the middle. And, it was a large statue, made of stone and perhaps six feet tall. One man, even two men, could not have carried it without great difficulty. The next morning on his way to work the man passed by the cemetery again, and the angel was gone.

On another occasion, an eleven-year-old girl passed by the church and saw a minister standing just outside of the door, welcoming people. She didn't recognize him, so she asked her mother who it was. From the girl's description, the mother realized that it had been a former minister who had died six years before.

I've never attended services at the Wildwood Baptist Church, but it must be a wonderful place to worship; no one wants to leave.

Not far away there is a farm, and there is a house on the farm where, in the early 1940s, an elderly woman lived. She loved to grow roses—yellow roses—and everyone in the neighborhood was blessed, because she freely shared them. In fact, the woman was quite well-known around the area because of those yellow roses, which were always beautiful and robust and healthy. Then the woman died, and, strangely, the roses died, too. Several people tried through the years after her death to revive them, and to grow other roses in the same beds. No one was ever successful.

In 1944 an old man moved into the same house and complained of a woman who washed dishes at his sink and sang loudly. She sang mostly hymns, and she had a good voice, but the man got tired of it and finally moved. Of course, no woman was ever there.

In the 1960s a couple moved into the house and soon after told a neighbor who had lived close by for a long time that they often heard footsteps in one room or another. Also, every night around eleven o'clock they heard two loud thumps in a back bedroom. The neighbor explained that an elderly bachelor had lived there several years before and had died in the place. It had been his habit to retire around eleven, and he slept in the back bedroom. Perhaps, he was still there, and the thumps were his shoes hitting the floor when he took them off.

In the southeast corner of the farm there once was an old barn and a house nearby. At the time, in 1954, it was a chicken farm, and the couple who owned it often worked late into the night, getting all their chores done. One night, around eleven thirty, just after they had finished their work, they were sitting at the kitchen table having a final cup of coffee and discussing the day's events and the next day's work, when they heard a horse outside. From the sound of the hoof beats it seemed to be running toward the house from the old barn, although there were no animals there; it was no longer in use. The man grabbed his flashlight and went out to catch the horse. There was nothing there. The next morning he and his wife went out to look for footprints and found nothing, not one track. This happened several times while the couple owned the farm, and no one ever found any tracks or saw a horse.

Also, from time to time the same couple heard what sounded like opera singing coming from a trailer right next to the farm. The morning after the first time they heard it, at two o'clock in the morning, the farmer went to his neighbors to complain and ask that they keep their radio turned down that late at night. The neighbors denied playing the radio and swore they had been asleep. The music continued periodically for several years. In fact, visitors often came to spend the night, just to hear the phenomenon. No one was ever able to explain it.

Willie Watkins is a psychic and an author. She also collects dolls. One of her dolls is haunted. When you look at it, the doll looks like any other. It's just a doll, a normal battery-operated plaything, but this doll is different. It talks. It talks when the battery is turned off and even when the battery is taken out. There is more. It's not only that the doll talks, but when it talks. On many occasions it has warned Willie and other family members of danger. Once when her brother needed help, the doll spoke and warned Willie. Another time, when a prowler was in the yard, the doll started talking and told Willie of the intruder. Willie called the police who caught the man. Willie thinks her mother's spirit resides in the doll.

One summer Gay Rawley and Margie Godby were doing genealogical work in the Wildwood Cemetery, recording names, dates of births and deaths, and any information that could be gleaned from the headstones. One night shortly after they had finished their work, Gay was startled out of her sleep by a voice, not in a dream or her thoughts, a voice in her darkened room. Startled? No, she was terrified!

"You forgot the one in the middle. You forgot the one in the middle," the voice said. It was a man's voice. Clutching her blankets to her, she screamed, "What do you want? Get out of here."

The voice called again, "You forgot the one in the middle of the Wildwood Cemetery. You forgot the one in the middle of the Wildwood Cemetery."

Finally, Gay composed herself enough to sit up in bed and turn on the lights. There was no one else in the room. She had been sound asleep, but she knew she wasn't dreaming. She had heard a voice. Gay didn't sleep the rest of the night.

The next day she called Margie and related what had happened. Together they went back to the cemetery. By the time they arrived it was late morning and getting hot, but they went through it again, inch by inch. They found nothing they hadn't before. Gay started back toward the car, but Margie remained on the far side clearing away weeds, still looking for any stones they might have missed.

Part way back Gay stopped on the pathway to catch her breath. It was shaded and cool. She waited there for Margie, who finally trudged up the path toward her, wilted by the heat. Gay told her how cool it seemed on the path. "That's because you're standing on moss," Margie said. Gay looked around. Sure enough, the area was covered with moss. Then, she realized something. She was in the middle of the cemetery, a fact that was hard to determine because the place wasn't at all symmetrical.

They began digging and soon discovered a stone, as the voice the night before had said. Henry O'Barnum, 1828–1880. Gay says to this day that his was the voice that gave her the message.

THE $\mathscr{L}$IGHTHOUSE

Although the present St. Augustine lighthouse is hardly more than one hundred years old, the site on which it stands and the surrounding area have been in use by Europeans since the founding of St. Augustine and much longer by the indigenous inhabitants. The keeper's house is now the Lighthouse Museum, and Kathy Fleming is the curator. The lighthouse and keeper's quarters have a rich and colorful history, and there are numerous stories of ghosts.

*D*AVID AND MARYLINDA WOOD, friends of ours, live just fifty yards away from the lighthouse, so on a chilly February weekend we went up for a visit. We arrived on a Friday evening and, after a pleasant dinner and stroll through the Ancient City, we returned to the Woods' home and retired. For some reason I couldn't sleep. I had had a long, hard week, but I just wasn't tired, so I quietly got up, dressed, and went outside for a walk. The moon was almost full and the night was clear and cold. It was long after midnight, and the city was silent.

A thick stand of live oaks separated the Woods' home from the lighthouse, and as I walked down the unpaved street I passed a trail into the brush. That seemed to be the most direct route, so I turned onto the trail and headed toward the lighthouse. The cold, moonlit silence was eerie, and I grew a little apprehensive. Ten more yards and I was through the trees and near the base of the tower. I looked up to take in the full view of it. It was beautiful in the moonlight. All at once, in my peripheral vision I saw something move at the entrance to the lighthouse. I couldn't positively say it was a person, but it was far too large for a raccoon, cat, or dog. Slowly, I walked over to the entrance to look around. No one, nothing, was there, and the door was locked. Then, I walked around to the far side. Ten steps beyond the door on the south side of the lighthouse, I was jolted by a pocket of icy cold air which enveloped me, air much colder than the night, air as cold as a winter's night in the mountains of Montana. Frightened, I jumped back and got out of the pocket. I'd had enough and quickly retraced my steps back to the Woods'. When I climbed back into bed, I was sweating. The next morning I went to see Kathy.

Kathy descended the stairs and walked quickly down the narrow hall between the old cistern and the video room to the storage area at the far end. She needed some old files and was in a hurry. Flicking on the light, she went to a filing cabinet and rummaged around until she found what she was looking for. Reversing herself, she turned off the light and headed back toward the stairs. Her thoughts were on the papers in her hand.

Just before she reached the cistern, she caught movement out of the corner of her eye, and she froze. There, standing in the doorway of the video room, was a tall, gray shape. It was the shadowy image of a man. The hair rose on her arms, and her spine began to tingle. She was filled with—not quite horror—alarm. She looked straight at the figure, and it melted back into the darkness of the video room. Kathy, breathless, hurried upstairs.

That was not her first experience with a ghost, but it was her first direct encounter. Jamie Buddock and Matthew Arnold, who work in the gift shop of the museum, have almost daily experiences. Items in the shop get moved around and sometimes disappear for a while, although they always show up eventually. And music boxes start by themselves. In the video room, too, chairs are moved around and overturned. Nothing malicious happens, but the "presence" makes himself or herself known. Jamie and Matthew both have heard footsteps upstairs and down, but they've never seen the stepper. They have dubbed the ghost "Albert" because they heard a story about a man named Albert who died in the house. No one knows for sure who it is.

As the curator of the museum Kathy has heard all the stories. Supposedly, a man, possibly a keeper or an assistant, hanged himself in the basement. Then there was the daughter of a keeper many years ago who allegedly drowned nearby and refuses to leave.

There has been a tower of some sort on Anastasia Island since the very beginning of Spanish occupation. The first structure was a wooden tower, probably built not long after the Spanish occupied St. Augustine. It was burned to the ground in 1586 when Sir Francis Drake attacked the settlement. That first tower was soon replaced by another wooden one, which later was succeeded in the late 1600s or early 1700s by a coquina tower a short distance north of the present lighthouse. This tower served the Spanish well as a watchtower until 1763, when the British took possession of St. Augustine. The British continued to use the tower, raising its height and placing a cannon on top to alert the town of the approach of enemy ships.

In 1821 the United States gained possession of Florida and began using the tower as a lighthouse. Three years later a new structure was built on top of the old, and Juan Antonio Andreu was named the first keeper of the lighthouse, which originally carried a lard-burning lantern and fourteen-inch reflectors on its top. A revolving light later replaced the old lamp, and the beacon continued in use until darkened during the War Between the States.

The lighthouse was relit after the war, but by the late 1860s the tides had eaten so close to the lighthouse that it was in danger of falling (which it eventually did on June 20, 1880, during a high tide), and the Coast Guard began preparations to replace it. A Dr. Charles Ballard owned a large tract just to the south and agreed to sell. Incidentally, Dr. Ballard was from Albert Lea, Minnesota. Was this the "Albert" Jamie and Matt had heard about?

Allegedly, the terms of the agreement between Dr. Ballard and the Coast Guard were mutually beneficial. However, in typical bureaucratic fashion the government was unable to bring the deal to a close. In the meantime, the Coast Guard officer with whom Dr. Ballard had dealt was transferred, and the details of the "mutually beneficial terms" were lost. In the end and after a bitter feud, Dr. Ballard sold the land under terms not particularly beneficial, having lost the opportunity to sell on the open market for a much higher price. If Dr. Ballard does haunt the lighthouse, he probably has good reason.

The new lighthouse, the one still in operation today, was completed in 1874 and the keeper's house in 1876. Through the years many improvements were made. Kitchen wings were added to the keeper's house, landscaping was improved, coquina posts were placed on the boundaries, and in 1936 the light was electrified.

From its beginnings until 1955, the lighthouse was in the charge of a keeper. In July of 1955 Chief James Pippin retired as the last keeper, and the lighthouse was switched to automatic control. Mr. David Swain was the first caretaker of the "new" beacon.

The house continued to be occupied; Dan Holiday rented it from the Coast Guard from 1961 until 1967, when the building was vacated and shortly thereafter declared excess property. Mr. Holiday recalls that he paid thirty-six dollars per month rent for the place.

Mr. Swain lived nearby and continued as caretaker. Dan recalled many nights sitting in the old house listening to David's strange tales about the keeper's house and the lighthouse. "As I remember," Dan said, "David never moved around at night without a gun and a flashlight."

Once, the electric motor running the beacon had a series of failures. The first time it happened, David walked toward the lighthouse, intent on fixing the motor. It was the middle of the night and very dark. As he walked he heard other footsteps crunching the gravel behind him. He stopped and turned. The footsteps stopped. He could see no one. When he began walking again, the footsteps followed, very close behind. He hurried to the lighthouse and shut the door. As he ascended the stairs he heard a noise at the bottom. Still, he could see no one. Yet, when he climbed the stairs, he could hear footsteps clanking up behind him.

He finally reached the top and went in to check the motor. There were no loose connections. The bearings all were fine. There seemed to be nothing wrong. He turned the switch off, then back on; the motor started running as smoothly as a clock.

Now very edgy, he wasn't sure what to do. He had to go back down the stairs, but he was frightened. Well, he couldn't stay up in the lighthouse all night, so he took a deep breath and bounded down to the bottom. From then on he carried a flashlight and a gun. He knew the gun would be of little use against a ghost, but it gave him comfort.

The next night the beacon stopped rotating again, and again David hurried over, this time with flashlight and weapon in hand. As on the night before, he heard footsteps on the gravel and on the stairs, but this time he had a little more confidence. For three nights in a row the beacon stopped, and each time David found nothing wrong with the motor. Then, as abruptly as they started, the failures ended.

Dan tells of an incident that happened to him in 1965 when he was renting the keeper's house. One night a friend of his, the stage manager of the play *Cross and Sword*, came for dinner. When they finished it was quite late, so Dan offered a spare room upstairs. His friend accepted. During the night, he awoke and was horrified to see a young girl in a long, lacy dress standing in the doorway. She stood there for several minutes, her face expressionless. Then, without seeming to move, she just faded away. Next morning he told Dan about the girl. A chill ran down Dan's spine; David Swain had told him about a keeper's daughter who had drowned. Dan had been skeptical.

Several weeks later another friend from out of town came to spend a few days with Dan and slept in the same room upstairs. He did not know about the young girl who had appeared in the doorway, but the next morning he related the same story to Dan. Dan was convinced and later mentioned the episode to David. David just smiled.

In 1970 while the house was empty, a mysterious fire, perhaps an act of vandalism, destroyed much of the house. For ten years the house sat vacant, its ghostly skeleton a stark reminder of its history. Then in 1981 the Junior Service League of St. Augustine began restoration. During the work several mysterious events occurred. Beams fell for no reason; a scaffold collapsed; and one workman was seriously injured by a falling spike. Or was it thrown? After spending only short periods on the job, several workers quit and refused to go near the place. But finally the work was completed in 1988.

Perhaps the restoration was an exorcism, because the only incidents that have happened since has been nonthreatening. Perhaps Dr. Ballard or "Albert" was trying to make one last point. In any case, the ghosts who haunt the present lighthouse and the museum are all friendly, and Kathy, Jamie, and Matt would like to keep it that way.

CASTILLO DE SAN MARCOS
1672

LAPHAM

STORIES OF THE CASTILLO DE SAN Marcos abound. Construction began with ground-breaking on October 2, 1672, and with so long a history it is perhaps natural that legends would develop. Whether they are true or not cannot be determined, but, whether true or false, many of them are fascinating. One of the most interesting tales involves Colonel Garcia Marti, who was assigned as the garrison commander in 1784 at the beginning of the Second Spanish Period when Vizente Manuel de Zéspedes became governor.

Colonel Marti had a lovely wife, beautiful and much younger than the colonel. Mari Marti had but one fault; she had roving eyes. Also stationed in St. Augustine as a member of the colonel's detachment was a dashing young captain, Manuel Abela, perhaps the most handsome bachelor in Florida. He also had a serious flaw; because of his startling good looks and his silken tongue, he was remarkably successful in his intrigues with women. Thus, he was more arrogant than cautious.

And so, when the beautiful Señora Marti and the jaunty Captain Abela saw each other, sparks flew, and they threw caution to the winds. At first their affair was easy to hide. The British and Spanish governments existed side by side, and the colonel, as well as most of the more important men in town, was busily involved in the transition from the British to the Spanish government. Besides, Captain Abela was a master at seizing every opportunity. However, there were fewer than two thousand people in St. Augustine, and soon the rumors began to surface.

Eventually, even the busy Colonel Marti heard the stories and was alarmed. He couldn't believe his beautiful young Mari was seeing Captain Abela, but he had to know for sure. One evening he told his wife he had to meet with the governor. He told her that it would probably be a long meeting, so she shouldn't wait for him, and he left. Mari quickly sent word to her lover, Manuel, who hurried to her side.

However, the colonel, who had impatiently waited for the adulterers to meet, came back and burst in upon them. He was enraged, and, in fact, would have killed them both on the spot had it not been for his trusted sergeant, who was with him. He had them both chained in the dungeons of the castillo until he could decide what to do. For days he brooded over being cuckolded and having his masculine pride damaged. Finally, unable to stand the half-hidden smirks and whisperings, he strode over to the castillo and stood in stony silence as workmen walled up the dungeon with thick coquina stone blocks, to the terrified screams of his unfaithful wife and his traitorous subordinate. No one knows if the governor or anyone questioned the colonel about the disappearance of his wife and the desertion of his young captain. Certainly the workmen who built the wall must have said something to someone. At any rate, history does not record the event.

Supposedly, many years later, on July 21, 1833, an engineer broke through the wall and was overcome by the powerful, sweet fragrance of the señora's perfume. There before him hung two skeletons, chained to the wall.

Some say that even to this day there is an unearthly incandescence and the faint smell of sweet perfume emanating from one of the walls in the castillo's dungeons.

"I have a ghost in my house. I really wouldn't call her a ghost at all. She's just there. She's no trouble. I knew her when she was alive, a neighbor. She was killed in a car accident a few years ago and now hangs out in my laundry room. Not long ago a friend was over for lunch and, while sitting at my dining room table, told me there were no such things as ghosts. The lights in the house started going on and off, and a fuse blew. An electrician came out the next day and found a short in the dining room light. That could have explained the fuse problem, but why did it start so suddenly after my friend said she didn't believe in ghosts? Then, too, why did two light bulbs blow up in my hand before I even had them in the socket. That's not explainable. Yes, my ghost gets upset sometimes, but she's no trouble."

Bonnie L. lives on the south end of town in a large, rambling house built in the early part of this century. The previous owner was a popular man in St. Augustine, something of a celebrity. He had been a professional athlete and later a newscaster. He was a wonderful neighbor and a very kind person, respected and well-thought-of. He always had a twinkling eye and a smile for everyone, and you couldn't be around Frank very long without feeling good, regardless of the mood you might have been in.

He loved St. Augustine, and he loved his country; he was a real patriot, and on every national holiday he flew American flags of all sizes from his porch. And so, it was probably fitting that Frank died suddenly on the Fourth of July. His funeral was a big event in town.

His wife lived for several more years in the house and finally sold the place to Bonnie and her husband, who had known Frank and his family for years. Not long after they moved in, unusual occurrences started to happen. Bonnie would be standing in a room and suddenly be surrounded by a blanket of warm air and the feeling of another's presence. Small items would disappear and reappear. Often it seemed that someone had hidden them just for the fun of it. After a time Bonnie figured it out; Frank's ghost was still on the premises. He was responsible for all the mischief.

Once, while working at the kitchen table, Bonnie's mother was looking for her husband's death certificate, which she usually kept in a small strong box with other important papers. She couldn't find it. Exasperated, she called out in a rather harsh voice, "Frank, bring back that death certificate. I need it." Moments later she turned around and found the death certificate on the counter behind her.

Bonnie's husband has his office in the house. He is a very meticulous person and has a place for everything. He keeps his sunglasses on the corner of his desk in a case—except when Frank decides to hide them. Her husband will play the game for a while and search the room, but if he's in a hurry or he's had enough he just says, "Frank, I'm tired of this." By the time he reaches his desk, the glasses are back in the case.

Over the years Bonnie and her husband have developed a strong attachment to Frank and can't imagine life without him, but whenever anything is missing, they'll smile and say, "Frankie took it." And, usually, he has. Fortunately, he always brings everything back.

"My family has a beach house; I think my grandfather haunts it. A couple of years ago my friend, Emmy, was here, and her fiancé came down to visit. They had been engaged for over two years but hadn't seen each for six months; he was a Marine stationed in North Carolina. I asked my mom if they could use the beach house for a weekend, and, at first, she was really reluctant. Finally, she gave in.

"On Monday Emmy called me. She was indignant. I asked her what happened, and she told me the place was haunted. Windows shut; doors opened. Lights went on and off. There were noises all the time. They finally had to leave.

"I guess Grandpa didn't understand. He knew us; he knew we lived in the house, or, at least, used it often, but he didn't know this strange couple. Maybe he didn't approve of them being there because they weren't married yet. Who knows? Anyway, it's nice to know he's sort of protecting the place."

There's always a lot going on in St. Augustine. Almost every weekend there are activities of one kind or another. There are fishing tournaments, historical presentations, and parades. Seven or eight times a year there are "Night Watches." On Night Watch weekends, enactment groups from all over the state, and, in fact, from all over the country come to St. Augustine to relive history and to have fun. There are Spanish Night Watches from both the First and Second Spanish Periods, British Night Watches, Territorial Night Watches, and Civil War (War Between the States) Night Watches. Participants come dressed in period costumes and uniforms and can be seen at all hours of the day and night wandering around town. Their reenactments are very interesting to watch and are always informative. These revelers also provide color and gaiety to an already festive atmosphere.

The British Night Watch is usually held in December or January, and sometimes enactment groups are allowed to camp in the open field next to the castillo. During one recent encampment, a group of about thirty "British soldiers" dressed in eighteenth-century uniforms decided late one evening to cross the Avenida Menendez and have a beer at the Mill Top at the north end of St. George Street. It was a cold, dark, and foggy night. Now, there is a hedge between the parking lot and the Mill Top, and as these thirty soldiers passed through the hedge and were coming out of the fog, a slightly inebriated fellow came downstairs from the tavern. As he stepped outside into the cold, his blurry eyes in the dim light saw thirty eighteenth-century "ghosts" charging toward him. Realizing what he saw, he stopped, gasped—and passed out right on the spot! Fortunately, one of the "ghosts" was close enough and caught him before he hit the pavement. After they revived him, they took him upstairs for another beer and some good-natured ribbing, then made sure he got safely home.

"There's a man down on Bay Front who has this haunted house. I can't tell you which one; he doesn't want it publicized. It's haunted by a woman. I think she used to live there, and she's very territorial about it. Anyway, he has a large formal dining room, and he loves to have dinner parties. She apparently walks around during his parties and makes him quite uncomfortable, although he's the only one who can see her. But one time, one of his lady guests saw her and about choked. I think that was the only time. Anyway, one day someone broke into the place and was stealing the silver, when she appeared. Of course, she scared them out of their wits, and they crashed right through the dining room window. The police caught them just down the street."

"My brother, Steve, had just died in a tragic accident. It was really weird, because my Uncle Richard had died about three years earlier. We all went over to my grandmother's house the night before the funeral, and we stayed there. I was fourteen; the rest of the kids, except for my brother, Terry, were all younger. Terry was just thirteen months younger than Steve, and they had really been close.

"All the kids slept in one bedroom that night. I was sleeping on the floor. So I'm lying there asleep, and I woke up; something woke me up. Something or someone was in the room. The door was locked, too, because my grandmother is paranoid about some things. She has these huge locks on every door in the house. So, whatever it was standing there, I couldn't see a face, but I could tell it was a person. He or she was standing upright. I think, now, that it might have been my Uncle Richard.

"It was really weird. It went straight over to Terry and said, 'Terry, Terry, get up. Take your shower. It's time to go to Steve's funeral.' I was scared stiff. In a weak voice I said, 'Get out of here. Get out of my room!' The other kids started to stir. It walked over toward the door.

"Then it was gone. I jumped up and checked; the door was still locked. That was very strange.

"Then about three or four months later, I went to my grand-mother's house, which was very close to the cemetery where Richard and Steve are buried. I had skipped school and was over there watching soap operas. Gramma left to visit friends. Well, I was watching TV, and I kept hearing a noise, a rattling noise. I looked out in the hall and couldn't see anything, but it sounded like it was coming from the kitchen. Finally, I went down there.

"As I got near the kitchen I thought someone was in there. I got really scared. So, finally, I got up enough courage and went into the kitchen. I was standing in the middle of the room. Nothing moved. There was no sound. All of a sudden, the stuff inside the refrigerator started rattling, ketchup bottles and jars and things. Then it said, 'Hi, April.' The refrigerator said hello to me. I jumped out of my skin. I raced out of there so fast I tripped over a laundry basket, fell flat on my face, and raced into my grandmother's bedroom, locking the door behind me. As soon as I could catch my breath, I called my grandmother. 'Does your refrigerator talk to you, Gramma?' She said no.

"'Well, it's talking to me!'

"She talked to me a few more minutes and calmed me down some, then told me to go back and make sure the refrigerator door was closed. I was still scared out of my wits, but I went back to the kitchen. This time the refrigerator started rattling before I got to the door, and as I entered, it said hi again. I knew it was my brother because I could recognize his voice, and I said, 'Steve, I know it's you, but don't you ever do that to me again!' I guess he was trying to tell me everything was okay. He'd just been trying to get my attention."

IN CLOSING

*T*HIS BOOK BEGAN AS A LAMENT. MY WIFE and I were entering the Booksmith, the superb bookstore on the plaza in St. Augustine, as another couple was leaving. As we entered, Angie, the salesperson, was complaining that someone needed to write a book about the ghosts of this ancient city; the just-departed couple had asked about such a book. One thing led to another, and I accepted the challenge. I had always had a casual interest in ghosts and the supernatural and thought it would be an interesting project.

As it turned out it was more exciting than I could have imagined at times. Shortly after starting my interviews, taking notes, and collecting information, my computer started acting strange. For example, once I tried to pull a file off the disk I was using. It showed in the directory, but I couldn't load it. There was no reason; it just wouldn't load. I went to my priest for a blessing, and my wife bought me a small pewter cross to carry in my pocket. Inexplicably, the day after, the file loaded, and I had no more trouble with my computer.

Another incident occurred the day after I returned from interviewing Rick Worley at Catalina's Gardens. My wife and I were standing in the kitchen, both wearing shorts and rubber-soled sandals, peeling shrimp for a dinner party. I happened to lean against the dishwasher and received a sharp jolt of electricity. I jumped back, quite surprised. I wasn't wet or anything, and I wasn't touching any other metal.

I touched the dishwasher again, and, again, I got shocked. Then, cautiously, my wife touched it. Nothing happened. Later in the day, my daughter who lives near us came over and did not get shocked when she touched the machine. The next day my wife called the repairman who could find no electrical shorts; nothing was wrong with the dishwasher.

My brother did the illustrations for the book. A few days after I had sent him several stories, he called. He said he had just drawn the illustration used with "Gateway to Hell." He had felt funny while drawing it, tingling spine, hair standing up on his arms. In fact, it was spooky, he said. When he finished the drawing, he sat there for a few minutes just looking at it to make sure it was right.

Tom is a black-powder enthusiast. He collects antique powder flasks and other black-powder paraphernalia and has a particularly nice Confederate powder flask hanging on the wall of his studio. While he was looking at the drawing in question, the flask fell to the floor. He went over, picked it up, and examined it. The hook was still tightly secured in the wall, and the leather thong on the flask wasn't broken. The flask had hung on the wall for three years; there wasn't any reason for it to have fallen. He looked at the flask, then at his drawing and got a really eerie feeling. He immediately stuck the drawing in an envelope and took it to the post office to mail it.

These incidents may have been, and probably were, purely coincidental. On the other hand, my own mystical nature causes me to be quite superstitious about some things, and I choose to believe that forces beyond my comprehension were helping me keep my passion up for this project.

Sadly, in all my wanderings throughout St. Augustine, during the many interviews, and in all the time spent researching and just meandering around, trying to feel this ancient city, I never actually met a ghost face to face. The closest I ever came was my visit to the old Victorian house when I first started working on the book. Still, I'm not through with the ghosts of St. Augustine, and I surely hope they aren't through with me.

154